New Term

Malory Towers

Malory Towers

Enid Blyton

Enid Blyton

New Term at Malory Towers

Written by Pamela Cox

Based on characters and stories created by Enid Blyton

EGMONT

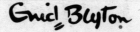

EGMONT
We bring stories to life

This edition first published in 2014 by Egmont UK Limited
The Yellow Building, 1 Nicholas Road
London W11 4AN

Text & illustration copyright © 2014 Hodder & Stoughton Ltd
ENID BLYTON ® Copyright © 2014 Hodder & Stoughton
Written by Pamela Cox

ISBN 978 1 4052 7276 6

1 3 5 7 9 10 8 6 4 2

www.egmont.co.uk

45850/8

A CIP catalogue record for this title is available from the British Library.

Printed and bound in Great Britain by the CPI Group.

EGMONT

Our story began over a century ago, when seventeen-year-old Egmont Harald Petersen found a coin in the street. He was on his way to buy a flyswatter, a small hand-operated printing machine that he then set up in his tiny apartment.

The coin brought him such good luck that today Egmont has offices in over 30 countries around the world. And that lucky coin is still kept at the company's head offices in Denmark.

Contents

Back to Malory Towers

'Darrell, are you and Sally absolutely sure that you don't want to come with Daddy and me when we drive Felicity to school?' asked Mrs Rivers as she buttered a slice of toast.

'Absolutely sure,' said Darrell firmly. 'I think that seeing dear old Malory Towers and knowing that I don't belong there any more would make me burst into tears, to be honest. Do you feel the same, Sally?'

Darrell's friend, Sally Hope, who was staying with the Rivers family for a few days, nodded. 'Exactly the same. I would like to go back and see the old place one day, but not yet. The memories of all the fun we shared and the friends we made are just too fresh.' Sally sighed heavily. 'I can't believe that our schooldays are over and we shall never go back to Malory Towers again.'

'You poor old things,' said Mr Rivers, looking up from his newspaper. 'Really, anyone would think that the two of you had nothing left to look forward to. But you're both off to university soon and a whole new chapter is beginning for you.'

'I know, and I'm really looking forward to starting university,' said Darrell. 'But it won't be as much fun as school.'

'I expect it *will* be fun, but in a different way,' put in her younger sister, Felicity. 'Just think, you'll have your own rooms, and no lights-out, and I bet you'll both be invited to lots of parties and dances, and –'

'And, who knows, we may even get a little studying done,' said Sally, with a laugh. 'It's going to be jolly hard work as well, young Felicity, so there's no need to sound quite so envious.'

'Oh, I'm not envious, Sally,' Felicity assured her, pushing her porridge bowl away. 'I absolutely *love* being at Malory Towers, and I can't wait to get back there.'

'And I suppose your eagerness to return to school has nothing to do with the fact that you'll be able to shake off Bonnie Meadows at last?' said Darrell slyly. 'My word, the poor girl won't know what to do with herself when you're gone.'

'Latch on to somebody else, hopefully,' said Felicity, with a groan. 'That girl has absolutely ruined my holiday. With all the towns in the country to choose from, why did her parents have to move here?'

'Felicity!' protested Mrs Rivers. 'That's not very nice. Especially as the poor girl obviously thinks the world of you.'

Felicity, who was getting a little tired of hearing the new neighbours' daughter referred to as a 'poor girl', rolled her eyes and said, 'No, she doesn't. Not really. She's just grateful to have some company of her own age, for a change. I'm sure she would have been just the same with anyone who had been kind to her.'

'That's the trouble, Felicity – you were *too* kind to

her,' said Darrell. 'You need to be firm with people, Bonnie.'

'I know,' said Felicity with a sigh, thinking that downright Darrell would have had no trouble in brushing Bonnie off. 'But I just couldn't bring myself to be unkind to her – in spite of the fact that she's such a drip!'

'That's what comes of wrapping children in cotton-wool,' remarked Mr Rivers. 'It would do young Bonnie the world of good to be sent to a school like Malory Towers, where she could mix with other girls and learn to stand on her own two feet.'

'But I thought that Bonnie was too sickly and delicate to go to school?' said Mrs Rivers.

'She may have been when she was younger,' said Mr Rivers, folding up his newspaper. 'But there's absolutely nothing wrong with her now – apart from an over-anxious mother, of course.'

'And Daddy ought to know,' said Darrell, referring to the fact that Mr Rivers was a highly respected member of the medical profession.

'Of course,' said Mrs Rivers. 'But I can't help feeling a little sorry for Mrs Meadows. It must have been dreadfully worrying for her when Bonnie was ill, especially with Mr Meadows being away so much. I suppose it's only natural that she's got into the habit of being over-protective.'

'Mother, do we *have* to spend my last precious moments at home talking about Boring Bonnie?' asked Felicity plaintively. 'Isn't it bad enough that she's been my shadow for the last few weeks?'

…n't mention her again,' said Mrs
…absolutely sure that you haven't left
…your trunk? And is your night case all
…ready?'

'…es, I've double-checked and I haven't forgotten anything,' answered Felicity.

'Good,' said Mr Rivers, pushing his chair back and getting to his feet. 'In that case, I shall go and start loading up the car and we'll be off.'

'I suppose *I* shall have to learn to stand on my own two feet as well,' said Felicity with a sigh. 'Now that I shan't have my big sister at school to look out for me. I shall be so lonely!'

Darrell laughed. 'Somehow I think you'll learn to stand on your own two feet very well. And as for being lonely – well, every time I tried to speak to you at school you were surrounded by your friends, so I daresay you'll be fine.'

'I'm so looking forward to seeing the others again,' Felicity said. 'Susan, and Pam, and Julie . . .'

'And June?' asked Sally with a quizzical look.

'Yes, even June,' laughed Felicity. 'I know that she can be troublesome, and outspoken, and downright wicked at times – but she's jolly good fun and she does make me laugh.'

Just like her cousin, Alicia, thought Darrell. 'Well,' she said. 'So long as she doesn't involve you in any of her crazy schemes, and get you into trouble.'

'I really think that June is beginning to change,' said Felicity thoughtfully. 'Remember how she knuckled down

4

to games practice last term? And don't forget that she saved Amanda's life!'

'Yes, June proved that she has good stuff in her,' said Sally. 'And no one could doubt her bravery. But she's one of those people who will always work hard if something interests her, or if she wants to prove a point to someone else. Once she loses interest, or has made her point and doesn't need to try any more – then watch out! Because when June is bored or has nothing to focus her attention on, that's when she starts stirring things up!'

Exactly like Alicia, thought Darrell, grinning to herself as she remembered some of her friend's more outrageous pranks.

Felicity laughed. 'Yes, you're right, Sally. Actually, I hope June doesn't change *too* much. I couldn't bear it if she went all goody-goody on us!'

'I don't think there's much danger of that,' said Darrell drily.

'June sounds a very strange girl, I must say,' said Mrs Rivers, who had been listening with interest. 'But it does seem that she has many good qualities – and Malory Towers is certainly the place to bring them to the fore.'

All three girls agreed heartily with that, but there was no time to discuss the matter any further, for Mr Rivers appeared in the doorway and said, 'Felicity, I've put your trunk and night case in the car. All I need now is you and your mother, and we can leave.'

Felicity leaped up excitedly to get her hat and coat, then Darrell and Sally walked with her and Mrs Rivers to the door. But, alas for Felicity, as they stepped outside, Bonnie Meadows was walking up the garden path, determined not to let her new friend go without saying goodbye. She was a pretty girl, small and very dainty, with enormous, soft brown eyes, brown curly hair and a little rosebud mouth. She also had an air of fragility and helplessness – or, as Felicity liked to call it, goofiness – about her.

'Oh, Felicity, I'm so glad that you haven't left yet!' she cried in her lisping, little-girl voice. 'I know that we said goodbye yesterday, but I *did* so want to come and see you off, and Mummy knew that I wouldn't be able to rest if I didn't get my way, so here I am!'

A snort from behind her made Felicity turn, to see her sister and Sally standing there with idiotic grins on their faces. She glared fiercely at them, then turned back to Bonnie and, in a rather too-bright voice, said, 'Yes, here you are! Well, Bonnie, it's been simply lovely spending the hols with you, but Daddy's waiting and . . . Oh, Bonnie, please don't cry!'

But it was too late. Tears had already welled up in Bonnie's big eyes, her bottom lip jutted out and, to Felicity's great embarrassment, she began to sob loudly. An expression of horror on her face, Felicity looked round at Darrell, who at once took charge of the situation. She came forward and put an arm round Bonnie's shoulders, saying briskly, but kindly, 'Come along now, Bonnie, there's really no need for all these tears. Before you know it the holidays will be here and Felicity will be home again. And I'm sure she'll write to you, often, won't you, Felicity?'

'What? Oh, er – yes, of course. Every week,' said Felicity, casting an anxious look towards the car, where her father was impatiently drumming his fingers on the steering wheel. 'Now, I really must go, Bonnie, or I shall be late on my first day back.'

She gave the girl a pat on the shoulder, then turned to her sister and said, 'I'll write to you, as well, Darrell. You will write back, won't you, and tell me all about how you're getting on at university?'

'Of course,' promised Darrell with a smile. 'Now off you go, or poor Daddy will simply explode! Say hello to dear old Malory Towers from Sally and me, won't you?'

Felicity ran to the car, Darrell's and Sally's goodbyes and Bonnie's cry of, 'I shall miss you so much, Felicity!' following her.

'Goodbye, Darrell! Goodbye, Sally!' called Felicity, sticking her head through the open window as her father started the car. 'Goodbye, Bonnie! I'll write to you soon.'

Then they were off – back to Malory Towers.

The journey was a long one, and to Felicity, eager to be back with her friends, it seemed to go on forever. Mrs Rivers had packed a picnic lunch and they found a pleasant spot overlooking the sea to stop and eat, but Felicity was so excited, and so impatient to resume the journey, that she could only manage a couple of sandwiches.

They drove on for another hour, then the car rounded a bend in the road and Felicity cried, 'There it is – Malory Towers! I can see it!'

Felicity felt a warm glow of pride as she looked at the

school – *her* school. Standing at the top of a cliff, Malory Towers was certainly a magnificent building, its four towers – one at each corner – making it look almost like a castle. Mr Rivers drove on, along a steep, narrow road and through a big, open gateway into the grounds of the school, which was thronged with excited, chattering girls and groups of parents. He had hardly brought the car to a stop before Felicity had the door open and was off, racing across the lawn.

'Felicity!' called her mother. 'You haven't got your night case. Felicity, come back!'

But it was no use. Felicity was now part of a group of laughing, gossiping third formers, all of them busy exchanging greetings and catching up on news.

'Look everyone, it's Felicity! Did you have good hols?'

'Hallo, Nora! Goodness, don't you look brown?'

'I say, isn't that Pam over there, with her people? Pam, come and join us!'

'Have the train girls arrived yet? My word, isn't it super to be back?'

It certainly was super, thought Felicity happily, looking round at all her friends. There was the big, good-natured Pam, the scatterbrained but humorous Nora, and horse-mad Julie, who had brought her pony, Jack Horner, to school with her. And now a slim girl, with short, light-brown hair and a turned-up nose, joined the third formers – Felicity's best friend, Susan. She slipped her arm through Felicity's and said, 'Shall we take our health certificates to Matron and find our dormy? Then perhaps we'll have time to go down and take a look at the pool before supper.'

'Good idea,' said Felicity. 'I say, where *is* my night case? Oh goodness, I've left it in the car. And I'd completely forgotten about Mother and Daddy! Wait here a moment, Susan, while I just go and say goodbye to them.'

With that, Felicity dashed off, back to where she had left her parents.

'Ah, so you've finally remembered us,' said her father, a humorous twinkle in his eye as she raced over to them.

'Sorry, Daddy, I was just *so* excited to see the others again,' gabbled Felicity, her words tumbling out. 'Susan's here, and Nora, and Julie's back, and she's brought her pony, and –'

'We quite understand, dear,' said Mrs Rivers, with a smile. 'I'm just glad that you like life at school so much.'

'Like it? I *love* it!' said Felicity ecstatically, hugging her mother.

Mrs Rivers hugged her back and said, 'Now, you will write once you've settled in, won't you? Just to let us know how you're getting on. And we'll be over to see you at half-term, of course.'

Having finished her goodbyes, Felicity grabbed her night case, and she and her friends entered the North Tower and made their way to Matron's room. Each tower at the school was like a separate house, each with its own dormitories, dining-room and Matron, and the girls came together in the main building for lessons. The girls from the different towers generally got along very well with each other, but there was a good deal of friendly rivalry, and every girl was intensely proud of her own tower, convinced that it was quite the best in the school.

There was a strange girl in Matron's room, handing over her health certificate, and the others looked at her curiously. She was striking, rather than pretty, with a long, aquiline nose, very straight, shiny fair hair and grey eyes, which were fringed with thick dark lashes that contrasted starkly with her pale hair. She would have been very attractive, but for her haughty, slightly disdainful expression. 'As though she has a bad smell under her nose,' as Susan remarked later. The third formers wondered who she was, but before their curiosity could be satisfied, Matron turned to greet them, saying with her beaming smile, 'Ah, more third formers! Well, girls, it's very good to see you all back again and I hope none of you is going to give me any trouble this term. I don't want any of you falling ill or having accidents. And, above all – *no* midnight feasts.'

'As if we would, Matron,' said Nora, with an innocent, wide-eyed look. 'We're going to be the best-behaved third form in the history of Malory Towers.'

'Apart from June, perhaps,' said Julie, with a laugh. 'I say, where *is* June? Have you seen her yet, Matron?'

'No, but I've no doubt she'll turn up, just like a bad penny,' replied Matron wryly. 'It's a wonder she and her cousin, Alicia, haven't turned my hair grey between them. Now, girls, let me have your health certificates – and woe betide anyone who has forgotten hers!'

But, fortunately, no one had, and as, one by one, the

third formers gave them in to Matron, the new girl stood to one side, watching them, Felicity thought, rather as one might watch animals in a zoo.

When Matron had finished, she seemed to remember the girl, for she said, 'I've a new girl here who will be joining your form, so you may as well take her with you and show her round a bit.' She put her hand on the girl's arm and drew her forward. 'This is Amy Ryder-Cochrane.'

Pam, who had been head of the form last term, took the lead and said in her friendly way, 'Pleased to meet you, Amy. I'm Pam Bateman, and this lot are Felicity Rivers, Susan Blake, Nora Woods and Julie Adamson.'

'Hallo, Amy,' chorused the third formers. 'Welcome to Malory Towers.'

The girl inclined her head in a way that was almost regal, and Felicity had to stop herself giggling. She didn't much like the look of Amy, but was determined to give her a chance. Being the new girl in a form where all the others had known each other for a while must be quite daunting, and perhaps Amy was just a little shy. So she smiled at the girl and said, 'If you come with us, we'll show you to your dormy. Matron, are we all in together?'

Matron picked a piece of paper up from her desk and said, 'Yes, you're all in dormitory number nine, along with June, another new girl called Winifred Holmes and Veronica Sharpe.'

Then she moved away to greet two second formers, while the third formers looked at one another in dismay, and Nora gave a groan. 'Veronica Sharpe! Don't say that *she* is staying on in the third for another term!'

'She must be, if she's sharing our dormy,' said Susan gloomily. 'Rotten luck for us.'

'Now, that's enough, girls!' said Matron crisply. 'Off you go now to unpack your things – and make sure that you put everything away tidily.'

'Yes, Matron,' chorused the girls, and they trooped out obediently, taking their night cases with them.

'I expect you must find all this rather strange, Amy,' said Susan kindly, as they made their way upstairs. 'But don't worry, you'll soon settle in. Have you been to boarding school before?'

'Of course,' answered Amy in rather an affected tone. 'I went to Highcliffe Hall, and it was simply first-class. One of the best schools in the country, and frightfully exclusive.'

The listening third formers, who thought that there was no better school in the country than their own beloved Malory Towers, raised their eyebrows at this and, pushing open the door of the dormitory, Felicity said coolly, 'If it's so marvellous, what made you leave and come here?'

Amy thought quickly. She couldn't tell the truth, of course – which was that her father had decided that she had become far too conceited and stuck-up for her own good since she started at Highcliffe Hall! And that the only way to bring her down to earth was for her to attend a good, sensible school, whose pupils learned the things that mattered. Instead she said, 'Oh, the school was so far away from my home that it was difficult for Mummy and Daddy to visit at half-term. Malory Towers is much nearer for them, so I suppose that's *one* advantage it has over my old school, anyway.' Amy followed the others into the dormitory as she spoke and looked round, wrinkling her nose in distaste. 'Goodness, it's awfully cramped in here,' she complained, putting her night case on one of the beds. 'At Highcliffe there were only four girls to a dormitory, so we had plenty of space to put our things. And I don't think much of the way this room has been decorated.'

And the girls didn't think much of Amy! They wanted to like her, and to make her feel welcome at Malory Towers, but, really, she was making it terribly difficult. Didn't she realise that it simply wasn't done for a new girl to criticise everything like this?

'Well, I'm sorry if our standards don't match up to those of Highcliffe Hall,' Felicity spoke up, looking coldly at the new girl. 'But I, for one, think it's a very nice room!'

'Hear, hear!' chorused the others.

And indeed it *was* a very nice dormitory. Despite Amy's scornful words, there was plenty of room for all the girls. Each one had a little cabinet beside her bed, in which she could keep all her personal belongings, as well as a small wardrobe. The beds had pretty green, floral patterned bedspreads, which matched the curtains at the big window, from where there was a splendid view of the beautiful gardens. One of the beds already had a pair of slippers placed neatly beside it, and there was a book on top of the little cabinet. The girls guessed that they belonged to Veronica, and wondered where she was.

'How I hate unpacking,' sighed Nora, opening her night

case. 'Thank goodness our trunks aren't brought up until tomorrow, because I simply couldn't face having to put everything away tidily on my first day back.'

A frown crossed Amy's haughty little face as she said, 'Don't tell me that we actually have to unpack our trunks ourselves? Why, at Highcliffe Hall each dormitory had a maid, who did all our unpacking, and looked after our clothes, and made our beds.'

Pam, who was bending over her night case, looked up and said, 'Well, I'm afraid there are no maids to unpack for you here, Amy. We have to do *everything* ourselves.'

'That's right,' said Nora, nodding solemnly. 'It's a hard life, but you'll soon get used to it. The dressing-bell goes at five o'clock sharp, and after we've washed – in cold water, of course – we must sweep the floor and make sure that everything is spick and span in here.'

The girls had to force down a laugh as they watched poor Amy, who looked as if she was about to faint! Then Felicity, with a very serious expression indeed, went on, 'After that, Matron comes in to do her inspection, and if everything isn't exactly right it's bread and water for breakfast. If we're lucky!'

This was too much for Nora, who gave one of her explosive snorts of laughter and Amy, realising at last that she was being teased, flushed bright red and glared furiously at the third formers. But she had no time to retort, for the door was pushed open, and a girl with wicked, narrow dark eyes and a cheeky expression burst in. June was back!

New friends and an old enemy

At once a perfect hubbub broke out, and the newcomer found herself surrounded. June might be stubborn, outspoken and malicious, but she also had the kind of daring and boldness that the others envied and that, along with her talent for playing the most amazing tricks and a wicked sense of humour, meant that she was extremely popular.

'June, you're back! How marvellous!'

'Did you come on the train? We wondered where you were.'

'Hope you've brought plenty of jokes and tricks with you.'

June grinned. 'You bet I have! And I've brought something else too – a new member of the third form.'

She stood aside and, for the first time, the girls realised that someone had entered the room behind her. The new girl had a short, boyish cap of pale hair, laughing blue eyes and a friendly, open face. The girls liked the look of her at once, and thought how different she was from Amy when she grinned round and said, 'Hallo everyone, I'm Freddie Holmes. Well, actually I'm Winifred Holmes, but everyone calls me Freddie, so I hope that you will too. June has been telling me all about Malory Towers, and I simply can't tell you how happy I am to be here.'

'Oh, do you two know one another, then?' asked Julie.

'We met on the train,' said June, slipping her arm through Freddie's. 'Miss Peters was there, too, and, knowing what a kind soul I am, asked me to take Freddie under my wing.'

Felicity looked sharply at June, knowing that – at times – she could be extremely *un*kind. But there was no trace of malice in the girl's expression now. She looked happy to be back at Malory Towers, and happy to have made a new friend.

Amy, meanwhile, had been very much in the background – and she wasn't happy about it! She wasn't the slightest bit interested in June and Freddie – or any of the others, for that matter. But she did like being the centre of attention, and didn't at all care to be ignored like this. She hadn't wanted to come to this stupid school, but as she was stuck with it, she meant to make everyone sit up and take notice. At Highcliffe Hall everyone had admired Amy's aristocratic looks, envied her expensive possessions and hung on her every word as she boasted about her wealthy, well-connected family. And she had thrived on their admiration and envy, for these things were extremely important to her. Although the Malory Towers girls seemed much more sensible and down-to-earth than those at Highcliffe Hall, Amy had no doubt at all that she would soon become a source of great admiration to them, too.

Eager to take centre stage, she opened her night case

and, with much groaning and sighing, began pulling things out and tossing them on to her bed. If she made enough fuss, perhaps one of the others would offer to unpack her trunk when it was brought up tomorrow! She gave a particularly loud sigh and June, who was extremely shrewd and very good at sizing people up, stared at her and said in an amused voice, 'And who have we here?'

'Oh, June, this is Amy Ryder-Cochrane,' said Felicity. 'Another new girl.'

'I'm afraid Amy is having a little trouble adjusting to our ways,' put in Susan, giving June a meaningful look. 'Her old school was *very* exclusive, you see. One of the best in the country, so she tells us.'

'Dear me,' said June smoothly, walking over to Amy. 'What a come-down for you having to rough it with us at Malory Towers.'

Amy looked at June suspiciously. Was she being sarcastic? The others were in no doubt at all, and waited with bated breath for the new girl to feel the full force of June's sharp tongue. But kind-hearted Pam didn't feel that it was fair to give Amy too hard a time on her first day, and stepped forward, asking, 'Have we time to show Amy and Freddie round a bit before tea?'

Susan looked at her watch and answered, 'There isn't time to show them everything, but perhaps we can take a quick look at the swimming-pool.'

'And the stables,' put in Julie. 'I must see how Jack has settled in.'

'Jack?' repeated Freddie, looking puzzled.

'Jack is Julie's pony,' explained Felicity. 'His full name is Jack Horner, but his friends call him Jack.'

'A pony at school!' exclaimed Freddie. 'My word, how super. I'm simply dying to see him, and the swimming-pool, and . . . oh, everything!'

'Well, buck up and get your night case unpacked,' said Felicity. 'You too, June, otherwise we shan't have time to show the new girls round at all.'

The two latecomers quickly unpacked, then June noticed that there were two spare beds.

'Someone seems to be missing,' she said.

'Well, there are normally ten to a dormitory, but there are only nine of us this year,' said Felicity. 'That's why there's a spare bed.'

'But there are only eight of us here,' said June. Then she pointed towards the bed with the slippers beside it and asked, 'Who's sleeping there?'

'Oh, of course, you won't have heard, June,' said Pam. 'We're to have the pleasure of Veronica Sharpe's company this term.'

'How lovely for us,' said June, pulling a face. 'Just what we need in the third form – a sly, spiteful little snob. I know that none of the old third formers could stand her.'

'You had better watch your step, Felicity,' said Julie, with a frown. 'Do you remember how your sister, Darrell, caught her snooping around in the sixth's common-room last term?'

'Yes, I remember,' said Felicity, with a grin. 'Darrell made her write an essay on respecting one's elders, and got her to read it out to the whole of the sixth form. But I don't see what that's got to do with me!'

'Well, Veronica was simply furious with Darrell, but was too much of a coward to try and get back at her,' said Julie. 'And if she's still holding a grudge, she might try to take it out on you.'

'Well, if she tries any of her mean tricks on Felicity, she'll have the whole of the third form to deal with,' said Susan loyally.

'She certainly will,' agreed Pam. 'But come on, let's not waste any more of our time discussing Veronica. We'll take a look in at our new common-room, then go down to the swimming-pool.'

And, chattering at the top of their voices, the girls left the dormitory and made their way downstairs.

As their voices faded away, the door of the bathroom at the end of the dormitory opened and someone stepped out – Veronica Sharpe!

Veronica hadn't meant to listen in on the others – at first. She had just finished washing her hands in the bathroom when she had heard the third formers enter, and she fully intended to make her presence known and say hallo to them. Then she had overheard Amy's remarks and been most impressed by how grand the new girl sounded. Wouldn't it be fine to have a girl like that for a friend, she thought – someone right out of the top drawer! As she listened, it quickly became clear that the others weren't impressed by Amy at all – and that suited Veronica just fine, for it meant that she would have no competition. Veronica had always found it difficult to make friends at school, but she couldn't see that it was due to her own sly, rather spiteful nature. She preferred to tell herself that none of the girls at Malory Towers were good enough to become her friend. But now, here was someone who *was* good enough.

She took a step towards the door, then stopped suddenly, as a thought occurred to her. If she joined the others now they would know that she had overheard them, and would realise that she was only trying to befriend Amy because she was grand and wealthy. No, better to stay hidden for the time being. Veronica decided that she would go all out to win Amy over at teatime, then nobody could accuse her of wanting to be friends with the new girl for the wrong reasons. Pleased with herself, the girl tiptoed across to the bathroom door, listening for all she was worth. A sneer crossed her face when she heard the others greet that horrid June. How Veronica disliked that girl – and how she would love to take her down a peg or two! Well, when Miss Peters announced that she was to be head-girl of the third form tomorrow, she would do exactly that! Veronica almost shivered with excitement at the thought. She was *sure* to be head-girl, for she had been in the third form for one term already – and wouldn't she enjoy lording it over the others! *And* she was going to have the richest girl in the form for her friend. The term was really getting off to a good start.

Then Veronica heard her own name mentioned, and pressed her ear even closer to the door. The smug smile slid from her face as she heard what the others thought of her. Sly, sneaky, spiteful and a coward. Tears of anger and self-pity sprang to her eyes and she turned red with humiliation. The mean beasts! Not for a moment did it occur to Veronica that it was her own behaviour in the past that had made the third formers despise her. Nor did it cross her mind that the girls were only speaking the truth. She *did* still bear a grudge against that high and mighty Darrell Rivers, and had spent many pleasant hours during the holidays thinking up ways to get back at her through her younger sister. The third formers' scornful words might have made another girl stop and think, and perhaps decide to change her ways. But Veronica only felt even more determined to get back at Felicity for her disgrace last term.

Part of her wanted to storm out of the bathroom and confront the third formers. But that would only end in Veronica feeling even more humiliated, for then they would know that she had been eavesdropping. And what would Amy think of her then? No, she needed to keep a cool head and not act rashly. It was a relief when she heard the others leave, and could emerge from her hiding place.

With the dormitory all to herself, Veronica was quite unable to resist the urge to do a little snooping. That must be Felicity's bed, over by the window, for there was a framed photograph on the cabinet of Felicity, Darrell and their parents. The family looked very happy, all of them smiling widely, but Veronica felt very sour indeed as she picked it up, fighting an impulse to throw it to the ground and smash it. But that would be a mistake, for the others would instantly suspect her. This was typical of Veronica, who only saw things as they affected her. She didn't think that it would be *wrong* to destroy another girl's belongings – merely that it would be a shame if she was caught out!

Carefully she replaced the photograph and walked over to the bed next to hers, wondering who the occupant was. A bottle of expensive French perfume stood on the cabinet and a very pretty pink dressing-gown had been placed, folded very carefully, on the bed. Veronica ran her hand over it, thrilled to discover that it felt like real silk. This must be Amy's bed, for surely no other third former would have such exquisite belongings. What a bit of luck that the new girl had chosen the bed next to hers! Instantly, Veronica's ill humour disappeared. There would be plenty of time for her to teach Felicity a lesson – after all, she had the whole term ahead of her. For now she meant to concentrate on making a friend of Amy.

The rest of the third form, meanwhile, were happily showing off their school to the new girls.

It was a real pleasure, thought Felicity, to show Freddie round. The new girl seemed genuinely thrilled to be at Malory Towers, and exclaimed with delight at everything, reminding Felicity very much of the way she had felt on her first day. Amy, however, turned her rather large nose up at everything.

'Don't we have our own studies here?' she asked, surprised and displeased, as they looked in at the cosy common-room. 'We did at Highcliffe Hall, and we were allowed to decorate them just as we pleased.'

'You'll have to make do with a common-room now, Amy,' said June. 'I'm sure you'll think that it suits the rest of us down to the ground – a common-room for common girls!'

The others laughed, but Amy scowled and turned away.

At the stables, Freddie went into ecstasies over Jack, making a great fuss of him and begging Julie to let her ride him one day. But Amy refused to go near him, complaining that the smell of the stables made her feel sick.

When they reached the pool, Freddie's eyes lit up and she exclaimed, 'Oh, how lovely it looks! So inviting! I could dive in right now.'

'Well, I shouldn't dive in with your clothes on, Freddie,' laughed Nora. 'Or you'll get into a row with Matron. But the weather is still quite warm for September, so you may get the chance to go for a dip later in the week.'

The Malory Towers girls were very proud of their beautiful, natural swimming-pool, which was hollowed out of rocks and filled by the sea as the tide ebbed and flowed. Amy, though, barely glanced at it, merely remarking haughtily, 'We had a magnificent indoor pool at Highcliffe Hall. It was heated, which meant that we could swim in the winter months too.'

Even good-natured Pam became exasperated with her, and muttered crossly to Felicity and June, 'She'll be going for a swim sooner than she thinks, if she doesn't shut up. I'm just itching to shove her in!'

'Be patient, Pam,' laughed June. 'I've one or two tricks up my sleeve and it won't be too long before dear Amy learns that pride comes before a fall!'

As the third formers walked back to North Tower, they

spotted two sixth formers coming towards them, and Susan said, 'Look, it's Kay Foster, the new Head Girl. And Amanda!'

Amanda Chartelow had been in the sixth form with Darrell last term. She had been a superb sportswoman, but had annoyed many of the girls with her arrogance and superior attitude. But poor Amanda had learned a hard lesson when she broke the rules of the school and went swimming in the sea. The strong current had thrown her on to the rocks, and it was thanks to June that she hadn't drowned. Sadly, though, Amanda's injuries had put paid to her hopes of representing her country in the Olympic Games, or of taking part in any sport at all for a while, and the girl had gone through a very bad time indeed. It would have been very easy for her to have moped about, or become bitter, but Amanda had proved to everyone that her character was as strong as her body. Almost overnight, she had lost her arrogance, thrown herself into coaching the younger girls, and had made up her mind that, if she couldn't pursue a career as a sportswoman, she would train as a Games Mistress. Amanda had become a much nicer person and the girls, who had once disliked her so heartily, now admired and looked up to her. And they were very pleased to see that the slight limp, which had been a result of her injuries, now seemed to have disappeared.

Amanda greeted the third formers cheerily, then gave them some news which delighted them. 'Miss Grayling has made me games captain. So I hope all you youngsters are going to work hard for me, for I shall be a real tyrant!' But there was a broad grin on Amanda's face, and the third formers knew that she would never be a tyrant again.

'Oh, Amanda, that is good news!' said Felicity. 'I must write and tell Darrell. She'll be absolutely thrilled for you.'

'How's the leg?' asked June, who had even more interest than the others in the sixth former. She, more than anyone, had clashed with the old Amanda. But June's act of bravery in saving her life had created a bond between them, and now they had a great mutual respect for one another.

'Getting better,' said Amanda. 'My parents made sure that I spent the holidays resting and, although it nearly drove me mad at the time, it really has done me good. I still shan't be playing any sport for a bit, but the doctor says that there has been no permanent damage. Anyway, that's quite enough about me – I suppose you've all heard that Kay here is the new Head Girl?'

'Yes, and I'm going to have a jolly hard time living up to the previous one,' said Kay, with a laugh. She was a tall, dark girl with warm brown eyes, a humorous face and a friendly manner. The younger girls liked her enormously and felt certain that she would be a worthy successor to Darrell.

As the third formers went on their way, Susan said to Felicity, 'Well, I think Miss Grayling has made two jolly good choices there. I wonder who will be head of the form?'

'I expect we'll find out tomorrow,' said Felicity. 'I wouldn't be surprised if it was you, Susan.'

Her friend laughed. 'That's funny, I was just about to say exactly the same about you.'

'I don't think Miss Peters will choose me,' said Felicity, feeling pleased that Susan thought she would make a good head girl, but quite certain that she wouldn't be in the running. 'I can be so indecisive sometimes – and I don't know if I would be strong enough to keep people like June in order.'

'Even the mistresses have a hard time keeping June in order!' chuckled Susan. 'I say, perhaps they will make *her* head of the form! There's no doubt that she would make a strong leader.'

'True. But she would lead us all into trouble!' said Felicity. Then she gave a sigh. 'I expect it will be Veronica. After all, she has already been in the third for a term.'

'I'd forgotten all about Veronica!' said Susan in dismay. 'Blow, we shall have a miserable time of it if she's head of the form.'

The first night

A most delicious supper had been laid out in the dining-room. Each of the long tables was set with big plates of cold meat, bowls of salad and delicious, buttery potatoes baked in their jackets. There was the most scrumptious-looking fruit salad with cream for afters and, as the girls entered, their eyes lit up.

Two people were already seated at the third-form table. One was Mam'zelle Dupont, one of the school's two French mistresses, and the other was Veronica Sharpe. The girls eyed her a little warily, but Veronica – eager to make a good impression on Amy – was on her best behaviour and greeted them with a cheery 'Hallo' and a wide smile. The third formers looked surprised but – thinking that perhaps the girl had decided to turn over a new leaf, and determined to give her a chance – smiled back. Veronica glanced at the two new girls, noting that one of them was laughing and joking with June. That must be Freddie, so the girl with the straight, shiny hair and rather aloof expression must be Amy. She was standing slightly apart from the others and, although she would never have admitted it, feeling a little lost as they all seated themselves. So when Veronica touched her arm and said in a friendly way, 'You must be new. Why don't you have the seat next to mine?' she felt extremely grateful.

'Ah, welcome back *mes petites*!' cried plump little Mam'zelle Dupont, smiling around. 'How good it is to see you all again – Felicity, Susan, Pam, Julie – ah, and the dear Nora! I see that we have some new girls, also. The good Miss Potts told me to expect you,' went on Mam'zelle. 'And she told me your names. I know that one of you is called Winifred, and that –'

'It's Freddie, Mam'zelle, not Winifred,' June corrected her, helping herself to a jacket potato.

'Always you interrupt, June,' said Mam'zelle, looking put out. 'And I know that you are pulling my foot, for Freddie is a boy's name.'

'You mean pulling your leg, Mam'zelle,' said June, with a grin, as the others giggled. 'But I'm not, honestly. She really *is* called Freddie – aren't you, Freddie?'

Freddie nodded. 'It's true, Mam'zelle. People only call me Winifred if I'm in trouble.'

It seemed very odd to Mam'zelle that this girl should want to be known by a boy's name, but she had been teaching at Malory Towers long enough to know that English girls could be very eccentric indeed. So she accepted this with a shrug and said, 'Ah well, I should not like you to think that you were in trouble, so I shall call you Freddie. And you, *ma chère*.' She turned to Amy, with a smile. 'You have an unusual name too, have you not?'

'Not really, Mam'zelle,' answered the girl, looking puzzled. 'My name is Amy.'

'Ah yes, but your surname, *he* is unusual,' said Mam'zelle. 'Miss Potts told me. Now, what was it again? Something from one of your English nursery rhymes.'

Mam'zelle frowned as she tried to remember, while the third formers looked perplexedly at one another and Amy said, 'But my surname has nothing to do with a nursery rhyme. It's Ryder –'

'Ah yes, I have it!' cried Mam'zelle, banging her hand down on the table and making everyone jump. 'It is Ryder-Cockhorse!'

The third formers simply roared with laughter at this. All except Amy, of course, who couldn't bear to be made fun of, even unwittingly, and flushed angrily. Even sourpuss Veronica had to hide a smile, but hide it she did, as she certainly didn't want Amy to think that she was laughing at her.

'*To see a fine lady on a white horse,*' murmured June, once the laughter had died down. 'Only Amy would never ride a white horse, because she wouldn't be able to stand the smell.'

Of course, this made the third-form table erupt again, the girls' laughter so noisy that Miss Potts, at the head of the first-form table, glared across at them, and Felicity said, 'We'd better keep the noise down. Potty looks annoyed.'

'Miss Potts,' explained June, seeing that the two new girls looked puzzled. 'She's the head of North Tower. Quite a decent sort, but she doesn't stand any nonsense. That's her, over at the first-form table.'

Freddie glanced across and caught the beady eye of a

rather stern-looking mistress, and looked away again hastily. No, Freddie decided, she definitely wouldn't like to get on the wrong side of Miss Potts!

'And over there,' said June, nodding towards the fourth form's table, 'is Mam'zelle Rougier, the other French mistress.'

Mam'zelle Rougier was tall, and as thin as Mam'zelle Dupont was plump. She also looked rather bad-tempered, and the fourth formers at her table seemed a little glum and subdued.

'Thank goodness we've got Mam'zelle Dupont at our table,' went on June, lowering her voice. 'She has a hot temper at times, but she's good fun and a splendid person to play tricks on. Quite unlike Mam'zelle Rougier, who has no sense of humour at all.'

Mam'zelle Dupont, meanwhile, had returned to the vexed question of Amy's surname, saying, 'It is a most unusual name, Ryder-Cockhorse. I do not think that I have heard it before.'

'Actually it's Ryder-*Cochrane*,' said Amy rather stiffly, as muffled giggles broke out again.

Seeing that Amy's feathers were seriously ruffled, Veronica seized her chance and murmured in a low tone, 'You mustn't mind Mam'zelle. She doesn't mean to offend – it's just that she gets things mixed up sometimes. As for the rest of the third formers – well, I wouldn't take much notice of them either. They have a very childish sense of humour, I'm afraid. Here –' she passed a plate of cold meat to Amy. 'Do help yourself.

The suppers here are jolly good, and I'm sure you must be hungry.'

Amy *was* hungry, and she took the plate with a word of thanks and a faint smile. Encouraged, Veronica began to engage the new girl in conversation, asking her a great many questions, showing enormous interest in her answers, and making her admiration quite clear. Pleased that there was at least one person in this horrid school who appreciated her, and delighted with the opportunity to boast about herself, Amy began to thaw and chatted quite pleasantly with Veronica.

June, on the opposite side of the table, was busily pointing out various girls and mistresses to an interested Freddie, but her sharp ears picked up snatches of the two girls' conversation. If she didn't know better, June would have felt quite certain that Veronica was sucking up to Amy because of her wealthy background. But Veronica hadn't been in the dormitory earlier and had only just met Amy, so she couldn't possibly know anything about her. Perhaps Veronica really *had* changed her ways, and was being kind and unselfish in putting Amy at her ease. But somehow June doubted it.

Mam'zelle Dupont, however, was quite taken in. Veronica had never been one of her favourites, but watching her now, as she went out of her way to make this new girl feel welcome, the French mistress began to think that she might have judged her a little harshly.

The bold, wicked June also seemed to be looking after Freddie, and Mam'zelle Dupont smiled to herself. Ah, they might be eccentric, with their jokes and tricks, and their strange names, but these English girls were good and kind at heart!

Nora, with her fluffy blonde hair and round, blue eyes, was one of her pets. When she covered her mouth suddenly to stifle a yawn, Mam'zelle Dupont cried, 'You are tired, *ma petite*! And no wonder. I am sure that you must all be fatigued, after your long journeys and the excitement of your first day back at school. As soon as you have finished your meal, you shall go straight to bed!'

There was an immediate outcry at this, of course. In fact, the girls felt pleasantly tired and wouldn't be at all sorry when bedtime came. But as for going up straight after tea, when it was so early, and there was still so much gossip to catch up on, and they wanted to make this precious first day last as long as possible – why, it was unthinkable!

'Only the first-form babies go to bed straight after tea,' said Felicity, rather loftily. 'We third formers are allowed to stay up until nine o'clock usually, although we have to go to bed at eight on the first night. And I, for one, am not going up a *second* before we have to!'

And stay up until eight they did, although many of the third formers felt their eyelids drooping, and Nora almost nodded off on the sofa in the common-room and had to be nudged awake by Julie.

'Come on, sleepyhead,' said Julie, hauling the protesting Nora to her feet. 'The bell for bedtime has just sounded, and you can't go to sleep here!'

'I say, look at those two,' said Felicity to Susan, as they

walked upstairs together. 'It seems as if they have become firm friends already.'

Ahead of them walked Amy and Veronica, still deep in conversation, and Susan laughed, saying, 'It seems right, somehow, that the two most unpopular girls in the form have teamed up with one another. Although I'm not sure whether this friendship will be good for either of them. But Veronica seems determined to stick to Amy like glue!'

'Rather like Bonnie stuck to me, during the holidays,' said Felicity, with a wry smile.

'Ah yes, dear little Bonnie,' said Susan, with a grin. 'I should think you were as glad to see the back of her as she was to see the back of me!'

Susan had come to stay with Felicity for a week in the holidays, and the visit had not been a great success. Bonnie, quite overcome with jealousy, had taken an instant dislike to Susan, and had done everything possible to make her feel unwelcome.

'As though *she* were my best friend and *you* were the one trying to come between us, instead of the other way round!' an exasperated Felicity had complained after a particularly trying afternoon, during which Bonnie had been openly rude to Susan. Luckily, the sensible Susan had refused to be drawn into a quarrel and had merely laughed at Bonnie.

'My goodness, how she disliked me!' Susan said now as they entered the dormitory. 'I couldn't help feeling a little sorry for her, though. It can't be much of a life not being able to go to school, and make friends, and share in all the happy, jolly times that most schoolgirls have.'

'Oh, Bonnie is quite well enough to come to school now,' said Felicity. 'But her mother won't let her. Honestly, Susan, I think that Mrs Meadows is quite the silliest woman I've ever met. If she didn't fuss over Bonnie, and spoil her so, she might turn out to be quite decent.'

'Well, thank goodness our parents had the sense to send us to a splendid school like Malory Towers,' said Susan. 'I simply can't imagine being anywhere else!'

Swiftly, the girls changed into their pyjamas, brushed their teeth, and climbed into their cosy beds, but June and Freddie, who were both thoroughly overexcited, continued to talk after lights-out.

'Can't you two shut up and go to sleep?' groaned a tired Nora. 'I'd just dropped off and now you've woken me up again.'

'Sorry, Nora,' said June. 'We didn't mean to disturb you.'

But, moments later, Freddie's voice could be heard again, followed by a loud snort of laughter from June's bed, and Veronica frowned to herself in the darkness. As she was to be head of the form, it was up to her to see that the two girls obeyed the rule about no talking after lights-out. It would be as well, she decided, to start as she meant to continue, and show these two that she wasn't going to stand any nonsense, so Veronica sat up in bed and said crisply, 'You two – June and Freddie! Get to sleep at once. You both know very well that no talking is allowed after lights-out, and if you disobey I shall report you to Miss Peters!'

Now, Nora wasn't the only one who had been getting a little tired of June and Freddie's chatter, for several of the girls felt annoyed at the pair for keeping them awake. In fact, Susan had been on the verge of telling them to be quiet herself. But none of the third formers intended to take orders from Veronica until it was announced that she was head-girl, and they rebelled at once.

'Sneak!' called out Julie.

'You're not head of the form,' said Susan. 'You've no right to tell us what to do.'

'Besides, I heard you whispering to Amy after lights-out!' added Felicity indignantly. 'And you only stopped because she fell asleep. Hypocrite!'

Veronica's cheeks flushed a deep angry red, and she hissed, 'Felicity Rivers, how dare you speak to me like that! I am the senior member of this form and I consider it my duty –'

'Pooh!' June interrupted her rudely, sitting bolt upright in bed. 'You don't have a sense of duty, Veronica. What you *do* have is an inflated sense of your own importance. Well, let me tell you, just because you've already spent a term in the third form, it doesn't make you senior to the rest of us, and it certainly doesn't give you the right to start dishing out orders. Only the head-girl will be able to do that, and I very much doubt that it will be you! Miss Peters knows you too well.'

Smarting, Veronica opened her mouth to make an angry retort, but just then the girls heard the sounds of footsteps on the landing, and the door opened and Miss

Potts stood silhouetted in the doorway.

'Come along now, girls, no more talking!' she commanded briskly. 'I realise that you're all excited to be back together again, but you'll be fit for nothing in the morning if you don't get your sleep. Who is head of the dormitory? Oh, no one, I suppose, as the head-girl of the form hasn't been announced yet. Well, Pam, as you were head-girl last term, I am putting you in charge for tonight, and will leave it to you to deal with anyone who breaks the rules. Goodnight, everyone.'

'Goodnight, Miss Potts,' chorused the girls, snuggling down into their beds as the door closed behind the mistress.

'All right, girls,' came Pam's low, pleasant voice. 'Miss Potts is quite right. We shall all be too woolly-minded to concentrate in class tomorrow if we don't get to sleep soon, so no more noise.'

'Whatever you say, Pam,' said June meekly, making the others grin to themselves. Apart from Veronica, who scowled fiercely. She knew what was behind this sudden – and most unusual – display of meekness on June's part, of course. It was her way of saying that she would accept Pam's leadership, but not Veronica's. For the first time, a doubt crept into the girl's mind. Could June have been right in saying that Miss Peters would not make her head of the form? It was true that Veronica had never been one of the mistress's favourites, but surely Miss Peters would not consider making one of these silly kids head of the form over her? Why, the idea was ridiculous, for none of them was fit to lead the others. Not the bold, brazen June, nor the scatterbrained Nora, that was certain. Pam had already had her turn, while Julie was so wrapped up in that horse of hers that she was quite unable to concentrate on anything else. As new girls, Amy and Freddie wouldn't be in the running, which left that cheeky little Felicity Rivers and her goody-goody friend Susan. Veronica curled her lip scornfully. As if either of *them* had the strength of character or the air of authority necessary to lead the third form!

Having ruled out her new form-mates as rivals, Veronica felt happier and settled down contentedly under the bedclothes. Miss Peters had a good deal of common sense and would not allow her personal feelings to influence her decision, Veronica was sure. The mistress would do what was best for the third form – and what was best, thought Veronica, would be for her to be made head-girl.

The new head-girl

Amy's first full day at Malory Towers did not get off to a good start. Veronica watched in admiration as the new girl brushed out her shining hair, before deftly braiding it into a thick plait, which she secured with a brown ribbon, to match the school uniform.

'You do look lovely, Amy,' gushed Veronica. 'How I wish my hair shone like yours.'

'I don't think that even *I* could look lovely in this dreadful uniform,' complained Amy, frowning at her reflection in the mirror. 'The one I had at Highcliffe Hall was so much nicer. We were allowed to wear –'

'Don't tell me,' interrupted June, who had been listening quite unashamedly. 'You were allowed to wear ball gowns and tiaras to breakfast.'

'I was talking to Veronica, not to you,' retorted Amy stiffly, scowling at June, before turning to rummage in a little jewellery box on her cabinet. From this, she selected a pretty charm bracelet.

'I say, Amy, you're not going to wear that in class, are you?' asked Veronica, frowning.

'Of course,' replied Amy. 'Why shouldn't I?'

'Well, we're not really supposed to wear fancy

jewellery,' Veronica told her. 'Miss Peters will probably make you take it off.'

The listening third formers grinned at one another, each of them thinking the same thing: that it was most unusual for Veronica to warn another girl that she was likely to get into trouble. Normally she would have held her tongue, for there was nothing that gladdened her spiteful nature more than watching someone else get into a good row. But Veronica was determined to become Amy's friend – her *best* friend – and that meant that she couldn't simply stand by and allow her to incur the wrath of Miss Peters without at least *trying* to stop her. Not that Amy seemed very grateful, for she merely shrugged and fastened the bracelet around her wrist, saying haughtily, 'What a stupid rule! I daresay Miss Peters won't even notice that I'm wearing jewellery.'

'*Rings on her fingers,*' chanted June in a sing-song voice. '*And bells on her toes. She shall be punished for wearing those!*'

The other third formers roared with laughter at June's clever rhyme, but Amy turned bright red. It would be just too humiliating if Miss Peters did send her out of class to remove her bracelet. Reluctantly, she turned away from the others and took it off, placing it back in the box.

Veronica noticed that the girl had placed a photograph on her cabinet and, in an effort to placate her, said brightly, 'Are those your parents? My goodness, isn't your mother beautiful? And how handsome your father looks.'

The woman in the photograph certainly was very beautiful, though she didn't look much like Amy, as she was dark, with a small, turned-up nose and big green eyes.

It was obvious that Amy had inherited her looks from her father, a most distinguished-looking man. His features were very similar to his daughter's and he had the same fair hair.

Amy cheered up at once at this praise of her parents and said, 'They are a good-looking couple, aren't they? You must meet them at half-term, Veronica. I say, wouldn't it be super if my parents hit it off with yours?'

Veronica listened to this with mixed feelings. On the one hand, she couldn't wait to meet Amy's beautiful mother and handsome, wealthy father. But on the other, she was quite unable to picture her own hard-working, down-to-earth parents becoming friends with the Ryder-Cochranes. Why, they had nothing in common with them at all! In fact, Veronica's parents could prove to be a bit of an embarrassment to her at half-term. Her mind working swiftly, she wondered if she could think of a way to put them off coming.

'Amy!' called Pam. 'It's almost breakfast time, so you'd better tidy your nightclothes away and make your bed before we go down.'

Amy, who had never made a bed in her life, looked rebellious, but the ever-willing Veronica was at her side in a flash, saying, 'You fold your pyjamas up neatly, Amy, and I'll make your bed for you.'

'Oh, no you won't!' said Pam firmly. 'Amy is quite capable of making her own bed, Veronica.'

'Really, Pam, I don't see what business it is of yours if I choose to help Amy,' retorted Veronica.

'It's my business because Miss Potts made me head of the dormitory – even if it is only temporary. And I don't see why Amy should get out of doing her own chores.'

Pam might be placid and good-natured, but she took her responsibilities very seriously indeed!

'But Pam, I really don't know *how* to make a bed properly,' protested Amy, looking at Pam beseechingly. 'I don't have the faintest idea how to fold the corners neatly, as the rest of you have done. Can't Veronica just show me how to do it now, then tomorrow I can do it myself?'

'Very well,' agreed Pam. 'But be quick, both of you, or we shall be late for breakfast.'

Amy turned away, so that Pam did not see the smirk on her face. Veronica had already boasted to her about how she was certain to be made head-girl, which meant that she would also be head of the dormitory. And if she chose to do Amy's chores for her, nobody would have the authority to stop her.

'Well done, Pam,' said Susan in a low voice. 'We're all going to have to sit on Amy good and hard if she's to settle down at Malory Towers.'

'Yes, but there's no point in the rest of us trying to get some sense into her if Veronica goes and undoes all our good work by running round after Amy, and telling her how wonderful she is,' said Felicity, with a frown, as she watched Veronica making Amy's bed. 'I simply can't understand it. Veronica is the very last person I'd have expected to put herself out for anyone, but she's really going out of her way to be nice to Amy.'

'Isn't it obvious?' said June, with a sneer. 'Veronica wants to be friends with the wealthy, well-connected new girl. Horrid little snob!'

'I would agree with you, June,' said Pam, thoughtfully. 'If it wasn't for the fact that Veronica struck up a friendship with Amy over tea yesterday – and she had no idea then that she is wealthy and well-connected.'

'That's right,' said Susan. 'Perhaps Veronica has genuinely taken a liking to Amy and really wants to be a true friend to her.'

'I don't believe that Veronica has ever been a true friend to anyone in her life!' declared the forthright June. 'She's only ever nice to people if it's to her advantage.'

'That's a bit harsh, June!' protested Felicity. 'I know that Veronica hasn't done much to give anyone here a good opinion of her, but she can't be *all* bad.'

June laughed. 'That's typical of you, Felicity. Always trying to see the good in people – even when there isn't any!'

And somehow June made it sound as if trying to see the good in people was a fault, and that Felicity was being rather naive and silly. Felicity felt put out, and was grateful when Susan laid a hand on her shoulder and said, 'You should be pleased about that, June, for it means that Felicity even manages to see a little good in *you*!'

June laughed at that, and went off to speak to Freddie, while Susan said in a low voice to Felicity, 'Never mind what June says – I think it's a jolly good thing that you're always willing to believe the best of people.'

'Perhaps,' said Felicity, with a wry expression. 'But it's not always easy. Especially with people like Veronica and Amy – and sometimes even June herself!'

Kay Foster approached the third-form table as the girls were finishing breakfast, and said in her friendly way, 'Hallo, kids. Freddie and Amy, can you come along to Miss Grayling's room with me, please?'

'Goodness, don't say we're in trouble already!' exclaimed Freddie, a look of dismay on her face.

'Don't worry, Freddie,' laughed Felicity. 'You're not in trouble. Miss Grayling always sees the new girls on the first day, and says a few words to them.'

'I'm sure you'll find what she has to say most inspiring,' said Veronica to a rather apprehensive-looking Amy. 'I know that her words had quite an effect on me. I'll come and wait outside the Head's room for you, Amy, so that you don't get lost on the way to class.'

As Kay marched off with Veronica and the new girls, June turned to the others and said in a low voice, 'Thank goodness Veronica's gone. Listen, everyone, I have a box of tricks in the dorm that my cousin, Alicia, gave me. I haven't opened it yet, so, as we have a little time to spare before lessons, shall we nip back up and take a look?'

'Ooh yes, let's!' cried Nora, clapping her hands together excitedly.

'That would be super,' said Felicity, pushing her chair back and getting to her feet.

'I have to go to the stables to see Jack,' said Julie,

frowning. 'Blow! I would have loved to see your tricks. Can't we go up and see them at break-time?'

'No, because I want to open the box when Veronica's not around,' said June, shaking her head. 'If she sees us all disappearing off to the dorm at break-time she's bound to guess something's up and come snooping.'

'Anyway, Julie, you saw Jack *before* breakfast!' pointed out Pam. 'I'm sure he's not going to pine away because you don't visit him *after* breakfast as well.'

'Yes, you can go and spoil him at break-time instead,' said Susan. 'Do come and see June's tricks with us now, Julie – it will be such fun!'

So Julie allowed herself to be persuaded, and the girls made their way swiftly up to the dormitory, where June pulled a cardboard box from beneath her bed.

'It's a pity Freddie can't be here,' said Felicity. 'She strikes me as the sort of girl who enjoys a good joke or trick.'

'She is,' said June, with a grin. 'Freddie was the form joker at her old school, and we're planning to team up and play all sorts of pranks this term.'

This sounded good, and the girls exchanged excited glances.

'I'll have to slip up here with her later,' said June, 'and show her what's in the box. Now, let's get the lid off and see what we have!'

The girls crowded round June, and there were a great many 'oohs' and 'aahs' as she pulled the items from the box.

'Good old Alicia!' exclaimed Felicity, as she picked up

an extremely realistic-looking rubber spider. 'My word, we can certainly give Mam'zelle Dupont a fright with this!'

But the most interesting item by far was a bar of perfectly ordinary-looking white soap, wrapped in pink tissue paper, with a label attached to it. As the others looked at it, puzzled, June began to read the writing on the label. Then she gave a crow of laughter and said, 'Listen to this! Whoever uses the soap will find that their face and hands turn a dirty, muddy brown about half an hour after they've washed. Oh, how super!'

'I should say!' chuckled Nora. 'We'll have to decide who to play it on.'

'I think I've already decided,' said June with a wicked grin. 'Can't you just picture our dear Amy walking into breakfast, completely unaware that she looks as if she's wearing a mudpack?'

The girls could picture it very well indeed, their eyes lighting up as they grinned at one another.

'Do it tomorrow, June!' begged Julie, but June shook her head.

'It's too soon. I always think it's best to save tricks until the term is a few weeks old and we're beginning to feel bored.'

'Good idea,' said Pam, as June shoved the box back under her bed. 'That will give us something to look forward to. Now, we'd better get a move on, or we'll be late and that won't impress Miss Peters at all!'

The girls made their way to one of the long buildings that connected the four towers, and found their new classroom. Amy, Freddie and Veronica were already there, as were some of the girls from the other three towers. The North Tower girls greeted them cheerily, then seated themselves. June was pleased to see that Freddie had managed to bag herself a seat in the coveted back row, and quickly took the one next to her. Felicity and Susan took the desks in front of them, while Pam, Nora and Julie found three seats together across the aisle from the others. Veronica and Amy sat next to each other, of course, at the front of the classroom, and as more girls from the South, East and West Towers came in, the desks gradually filled up. There was a babble of noise as the girls chattered away to one another, then Anne from West Tower, who was standing guard at the door, suddenly hissed, 'Shh! Miss Peters is coming.'

At once the noise ceased, the third formers getting to their feet as a mannish young woman with short hair and a rosy complexion entered.

'Good morning, girls,' she said crisply, setting the pile of books she carried down on the desk.

'Good morning, Miss Peters,' replied the girls politely as they eyed her with interest.

'Miss Peters is a good sort,' Darrell had told Felicity. 'But she has a temper. She won't stand for anyone playing the fool in her lessons, and if there's one thing that makes her angry, it's people who try to dupe or deceive her.'

She looks perfectly pleasant and friendly now, thought Felicity, as the mistress smiled round at her class.

'Sit down, girls,' she ordered in her rather deep voice.

'Now, before we get down to making timetables and giving out books, I am sure that you are all eager to know who is to be head of the form.'

A murmur of excitement rippled round the room and Veronica immediately sat up straight in her seat, a rather smug look on her face.

'Just look at Veronica,' whispered June to Freddie. 'My goodness, I'd love to see that smirk wiped off her face!'

'Quiet, please!' commanded Miss Peters, with a glare in June's direction. 'Well, this was a very difficult decision to make, but I have discussed the matter with both Miss Potts and Miss Parker, and we have decided that the head-girl of the third form is to be Felicity Rivers.'

Indeed, it had been a very difficult decision. Miss Peters and Miss Parker, who was the second-form mistress and knew the girls very well, had narrowed it down to Susan and Felicity, and found it very difficult to choose between them.

'I feel that both of them would make excellent head-girls,' Miss Parker had said. 'They are both sensible, trustworthy and kind-hearted. I really don't see how we are going to decide.'

Fortunately, at that moment, Miss Potts had entered the mistresses' common-room, and Miss Peters had asked her opinion, saying, 'As Head of North Tower, you probably know both girls far better than Miss Parker and I. What do you think?'

Miss Potts had sat down, remaining silent and thoughtful for a few moments. Then, at last, she spoke.

'There is no doubt that Susan has more confidence in herself than Felicity. However, I have always felt that young Felicity was a little overshadowed by her older sister. Darrell was so popular, and such a success at Malory Towers – especially in her last year, when she was Head Girl – that Felicity was always known as her little sister and never really came into her own. She has always been less sure of herself than Darrell, and less forthright in her opinions. Yet she is a very strong, determined little character and, now that Darrell is gone, I think that the time has come for Felicity to shine. I feel that if she was made head-girl she would certainly seize the opportunity and make the most of it. And I think that she has a great deal to offer the school. Of course,' she added, 'Susan would also make a fine head-girl, and the decision must be yours, Miss Peters.'

'I think that you are right, Miss Potts,' said Miss Parker, who had been listening to the mistress most attentively. 'With a little more confidence, I believe that Felicity could be as big a success here as Darrell was. She certainly has good stuff in her.'

'Very well,' Miss Peters said. 'Felicity Rivers it is then.'

'I'm afraid that Veronica Sharpe is going to be bitterly disappointed,' said Miss Potts drily. 'She is quite certain that the position is hers.'

'It never entered my head to make Veronica head-girl,' said Miss Peters, with a rather scornful laugh. 'I'm afraid that young lady has a lot to learn before she can ever be given a position of responsibility. She would have been a most unpopular choice!'

Felicity, however, was an extremely popular choice, and the classroom resembled a bear garden for a few moments, as the third formers congratulated her noisily.

'Well done, Felicity!'

'Jolly good show! You'll make a super head-girl.'

'My word, won't your parents be proud?'

June, delighted to see the look of horror on Veronica's face, cheered loudest of all, leaning forward and slapping Felicity on the back. 'Congratulations, Felicity! I'm so pleased for you.'

Only two girls remained silent. One, of course, was Veronica, who felt humiliated beyond words. To think that Felicity Rivers, of all people, had been given the honour that she had wanted so badly for herself. Veronica would almost have preferred that dreadful June as head-girl! And worst of all, she had actually boasted to Amy last night that she was going to be head-girl. Why hadn't she kept her mouth shut?

The other girl who was unable to speak was Felicity herself! For a moment, she thought that she had misheard Miss Peters as the mistress announced her name. Then Susan had given her a hug that almost pulled her out of her seat, the cheering and yelling had erupted, and she had realised that it was true. She, Felicity Rivers, was head of the third form! Felicity felt that she would burst with pride and happiness. She must write to her parents tonight – and Darrell, of course – and tell them the news! My goodness, how thrilled and proud they would all be! And what a super term this was going to be. Felicity vowed silently that she would be the best head-girl any form had ever had – even better than Darrell! Nothing would go wrong while she was in charge, nothing bad would happen and there would be no problems whatsoever.

But Felicity was wrong. The third form's problems were just about to begin!

5

A shock for Felicity

The first week of term simply sped by. Life at Malory Towers was full, busy and happy, so that the girls scarcely had a moment in which to be bored or homesick. But there were irritations too. Amy remained aloof and stand-offish, looking down on everyone other than Veronica, whom she graciously allowed to be her friend. As for Veronica herself, she had become more sour than ever since Felicity had been made head-girl.

'The two of them seem to have formed their own exclusive little club,' remarked Nora one day.

'Yes, though I don't know why Veronica thinks she's so superior to the rest of us,' said Julie rather indignantly. 'I saw her people last half-term and they are quite ordinary.'

'Veronica has become superior by association with Amy,' drawled June. 'Or at any rate, she thinks she has. And the more time the two of them spend together, the worse it's going to get.'

Felicity was in hearty agreement with June over this, and did her best to get the two girls to mix more with the rest of the form, but her efforts were in vain. Felicity spoke to Susan about it at tea one afternoon.

'I really feel that it's my responsibility to do something

about them,' she said in a low voice. 'They're awfully bad for one another. Veronica just encourages Amy in her belief that she's a cut above the rest of us. And as long as she has Amy for her friend, Veronica won't attempt to mix with the rest of us and will become even more unpopular.'

'Yes, but what *can* you do?' asked Susan reasonably. 'You can hardly order them not to be friends.'

'No, but I shall think of something,' said Felicity, with a determined set to her chin, and Susan grinned. She didn't doubt for a minute that her friend would do whatever she set her mind to, for she had always known that Felicity was a strong character. And now that she was head of the form, it was coming to the fore.

'I say, look!' cried Nora, who was sitting opposite them. 'Miss Potts has just appeared with a new girl. A first former, by the look of her, for she's only a little scrap.'

'Poor little soul,' said Pam, sympathetically. 'It must be awfully nerve-wracking to walk into a room full of strangers. Still, the first formers are a decent bunch and I daresay they'll look after her.'

Felicity and Susan, who had their backs to the door, turned curiously to look at the newcomer. Felicity, who had just taken a bite of fruit cake, choked, while Susan gasped.

'Bonnie!' said Felicity in horror. 'Susan, it's Bonnie!'

'Yes, I can see that,' murmured Susan, sounding less than thrilled.

For the wide-eyed little girl standing next to Miss Potts was none other than Felicity's neighbour, Bonnie

Meadows. At that moment, she caught sight of Felicity, and gave a high-pitched squeal of excitement, before daintily weaving her way through the tables to join the third form.

The girls stared at her in astonishment as she cried, 'Felicity! Aren't you surprised to see me?' Then, without giving Felicity a chance to reply, she went on rapidly, 'I missed you so much that I was quite miserable, then Daddy came home from one of his trips abroad and was quite worried about me, because he could see that I wasn't my old self. So he talked Mother into letting me come here, so that I could be with you, then he telephoned Miss Grayling and fixed it all up in a trice.'

Bonnie at last stopped to take a breath and June, who had been watching with a look of wicked amusement on her face, and had noted the shocked expressions on Felicity and Susan's faces, said sweetly, 'How nice for you, Felicity, to have another friend here. Do introduce us!'

'This is Bonnie Meadows,' said Felicity, pulling herself together. 'She's a neighbour of mine at home.'

'Well, that's excellent,' said Miss Potts, who had followed Bonnie over and arrived just in time to hear this. 'Bonnie will feel quite at home with you to look after her, Felicity. I shall leave it to you to help her settle in.'

Felicity, putting her own feelings to one side for the moment, quickly introduced Bonnie to the other third formers, and to Mam'zelle Dupont, who was extremely taken with this angelic-looking little newcomer.

'Susan!' she said. 'Please will you go to the kitchen and ask them for another plate for *la petite* Bonnie. And perhaps we could have some more cake, for I see that you greedy third formers have eaten it all up so that there is none left for the poor child. Sit down, *ma chère*, for I am sure you must be tired and hungry after your journey.'

As Susan went off to do as Mam'zelle Dupont had asked, Bonnie turned her sweet smile on the French mistress and thanked her prettily. Then she slipped into the seat that Susan had just vacated, beside Felicity, while Pam poured her a cup of tea.

The others, meanwhile, were sizing her up. Nora, who, with her deceptively innocent expression, wide, blue eyes and shock of fluffy blonde hair, was a long-standing favourite of Mam'zelle's, was none too pleased to see the French mistress fussing over this new girl. Pam thought her rather sweet, while Veronica considered her to be quite silly and childish. Most of the others thought that she couldn't be too bad if she was a friend of Felicity's, and were prepared to give her a chance. Felicity and Susan, of course, were thoroughly dismayed at this turn of events, and poor Susan looked most disgruntled when she returned from the kitchen bearing a tray of cakes and sandwiches.

'Thank you so much, Susan,' said Bonnie, looking up at the girl with round, innocent eyes as she set the tray down on the table. 'Oh dear, have I taken your seat?'

'It is no matter,' said Mam'zelle Dupont, quite failing to notice the hint of spite behind the sweetness. 'Susan, there is an empty chair at the second-form table. Bring it over, and you can sit next to me, then we shall be comfortable.'

Felicity, however, looked decidedly *un*comfortable, thought June, doing her best not to laugh. She turned her attention to Bonnie and asked, 'What school did you go to before you came here?'

'Oh, I've never been to school before,' answered Bonnie, tossing back her brown curls. 'I was very ill when I was little, you see, and the doctors said that I was too delicate to go to school.'

'Ah, *la pauvre*!' exclaimed Mam'zelle, her ready sympathy stirred. 'But you are quite well now, *n'est-ce pas*?'

'Oh, yes, Mam'zelle,' said Bonnie. 'And I'm so looking forward to starting school properly, and being with Felicity again.'

'You'll be able to make up a threesome, with Felicity and Susan,' said June, looking every bit as innocent as Bonnie herself. 'Won't that be super?'

Neither Susan nor Bonnie looked particularly thrilled at this idea, while Felicity groaned inwardly. She couldn't very well throw Bonnie off altogether – especially as she was head-girl, and it was her duty to help her settle in – but she certainly didn't want the girl tagging along with her and Susan all the time. Whatever was she to do?

After tea, Felicity and Susan took Bonnie up to the dormitory to unpack her things. Amy was there, searching through her cabinet for a book, and she glanced up when the others entered.

'There's only one spare bed, Bonnie,' said Susan. 'And it's this one, next to Pam's.'

Bonnie frowned, for she had been hoping to be next to

Felicity, but she said nothing and began unpacking her trunk, which had already been brought up by the handyman. She pulled out a pretty floral-patterned dress, which she had brought to wear at weekends, and it caught Amy's eye.

'I say, what a lovely dress!' she said, coming over to take a closer look at it. 'I have a very similar one that my mother bought me when we went on holiday to Paris. Where did you get yours from?'

'I made it,' replied Bonnie, looking pleased. 'It took me simply ages, but I didn't mind because I love sewing. Look, I made this one as well.'

'My word, you are clever!' said Amy, the genuine admiration in her tone astonishing Felicity and Susan, for they had never heard it before. 'These clothes are as beautifully made as the ones Mother buys for me. It must be dreadful to have to make all your own dresses though.'

'Oh, I don't *have* to do it,' said Bonnie. 'I told you, I love sewing – and it's the one thing that I'm really good at. Besides, if I make something myself, it means that it's truly exclusive and no one else has a dress exactly like it.'

'I'd never thought of that before,' said Amy, much struck. 'I do so hate looking the same as everyone else, don't you? Come over here, Bonnie, and I'll show you some of my things.'

Eagerly, Bonnie followed Amy, and Susan tapped Felicity on the shoulder, murmuring, 'I'm not particularly interested in the latest fashions, are you? Let's leave them to it.'

Felicity nodded and, unnoticed by the other two girls, who were now in the thick of a conversation about clothes, they tiptoed out of the dormitory.

'Well!' said Susan. 'It seems that those two have an interest in common.'

'Yes,' said Felicity, thoughtfully. 'In fact they're quite alike in many ways. Bonnie's not stuck-up, and she doesn't look down on people like Amy does, but she's awfully spoilt and vain.'

'Yes,' agreed Susan. 'When I stayed with you in the hols, I noticed that she was always doing her hair, or admiring herself in the mirror, just as Amy does. I say, Felicity, what are you thinking? I do believe you have an idea!'

'I was just wondering if we couldn't push Bonnie off on to Amy,' answered Felicity, with a grin. 'That would kill two birds with one stone, so to speak, for it would stop Amy and Veronica spending so much time together –'

'And it would mean that we wouldn't have Bonnie tagging along after us all the time!' Susan finished for her. 'It's a marvellous idea, old thing, but will it work? After all, Bonnie came here because she wanted to be with *you*, not Amy. And we both know how persistent she can be.'

The two girls had reached the common-room by this time, and they sat down together on an empty sofa. Felicity bit her lip, as she always did when she was thinking hard, and at last she said, 'Susan, I've got it! How would it be if I made a point of asking Bonnie to befriend Amy, as a favour to me? I can tell her that I'm a bit concerned that Amy isn't settling in very well, and that I'm worried she's getting too close to Veronica.'

'Bonnie's bound to agree if she thinks she's doing a favour for you,' cried Susan, her eyes lighting up. 'It's simply marvellous!'

'What's marvellous?' asked June, coming over with Freddie and sitting down on the arm of the sofa.

Quickly Felicity and Susan told the two girls their plan, and June grinned. 'Poor Veronica won't be too pleased at having to share her precious Amy. And anything that annoys Veronica is fine with me! I say, I hope that Bonnie and Amy aren't going to spend too long in the dormitory. I wanted to show Freddie my box of tricks before bedtime.'

But just then the door opened, and the two girls came in, chattering nineteen to the dozen.

'Just look at Veronica's face,' whispered Freddie. 'She doesn't look too happy to see Bonnie and Amy on such friendly terms.'

Indeed she didn't! Veronica was sitting in a corner alone, reading a book, and her lips pursed as Amy, instead of coming over to join her, sat at a table with Bonnie, and the two began poring over a fashion magazine together.

'She looks as though she's been sucking on a lemon!' chuckled June. 'Blow, I'd really like to stay and see what happens next, but we'd better go up to the dorm, Freddie, if you want to take a look at those tricks before the bell goes for bedtime. Felicity, if a row breaks out do come and fetch us!'

But there was no row, for as soon as Veronica got up to

join the other two, Bonnie left the table and came over to join Felicity and Susan.

'Amy's awfully nice, isn't she?' said Bonnie, ignoring Susan and addressing her remark to Felicity.

'Er – yes, awfully nice,' agreed Felicity, exchanging a glance with Susan. Now was the time to put their plan into action. 'Actually, Bonnie, I was glad to see you getting on so well with Amy, because she's a new girl too and hasn't really got to know many people yet, so –'

'But I thought she was friendly with that Veronica girl,' interrupted Bonnie.

'Yes, she is,' said Felicity. 'And that's the problem. You see, Bonnie, Veronica is . . . well, let's just say that she isn't a very pleasant girl, and she's awfully unpopular with the rest of the form. And I'm afraid that, by spending so much time with Veronica, Amy is cutting herself off from the rest of us and missing the chance to make other friendships. So, if you could be her friend too, I really think that it would be very good for her and I would be so grateful to you.'

The thought of being able to do something to please Felicity brought a sparkling look to Bonnie's eyes, and she glanced across at Amy and Veronica. Amy saw her looking and smiled, but the scowl that Veronica gave her was most unpleasant!

'Yes, I see what you mean,' she said at once. 'Of course, I'll be happy to do that for you, Felicity. But I'm only doing it as a favour, because *you* are my real friend, and no one else could ever take your place with me – not even Amy.'

Amy, for her part, had thoroughly enjoyed her little

chat with Bonnie. If she was honest with herself, she had little in common with Veronica, and didn't even like the girl very much. Really, she had only palled up with her because there was no one else, and Veronica did so enjoy listening to Amy's tales of her grand home and family. Veronica also made no secret of her admiration, and this was very pleasant to Amy. But it would be nice to have Bonnie as a friend too, and talk about things like clothes and hair-dos, which Veronica knew very little about. Amy thought that she would get Bonnie to make her one of her exclusive dresses too, just as she had got Veronica to make her bed every morning. Felicity had ticked the two of them off about it at first, but at last she had realised that she couldn't very well force Amy to make her own bed, and that if she put her foot down the girl would probably just leave it with the sheets in a muddled heap. And that would result in an order mark for the whole form, so in the end Felicity gave up, though she wasn't happy about it, as she felt that Veronica and Amy had got one over on her.

Bonnie lost no time in getting to work, going up to Amy in the dormitory as the third formers got ready for bed and saying, 'Amy, I simply must show you a new way of braiding your hair in the morning. I learned how to do it in the holidays, and I think it would really suit you.'

'I think Amy's hair looks lovely the way it is,' interrupted Veronica rudely, looking coldly at Bonnie. But Amy brushed her aside and said, 'Oh, thank you, Bonnie. I do so hate having to tie my hair back for school, and it's always nice to find a new way of doing it.'

And soon the two of them were gabbling away about hair-dos, while Veronica stood to one side, looking so put out that Felicity felt a little sorry for her. But soon it was time for lights-out and Felicity called out, 'Come along, Bonnie, into bed now. You and Amy can carry on your conversation in the morning.'

Within moments all the girls were in bed, most of them falling asleep immediately. Felicity had expected Bonnie, who had never been separated from her mother before, to feel homesick, and had dreaded that the girl would cry herself to sleep. But there wasn't a peep out of her, much to Felicity's surprise and relief.

But it was some time before Felicity herself managed to get to sleep, for Bonnie turning up so unexpectedly had really shaken her. And what if her plan to get the girl to chum up with Amy failed? Veronica certainly wouldn't want Bonnie tagging along, and would do her best to push her out. Then Bonnie would follow Felicity around like a lost puppy, making her friendship with Susan difficult, and life at Malory Towers much less enjoyable. Felicity sighed and turned over in her bed. Blow! *Why* did Bonnie have to turn up now? Just as things seemed to be going so well!

6

The new girls settle in

The three new girls each settled down in their own way. Freddie had a quick brain and could have done extremely well at lessons, but she preferred to follow June's lead and put her brains to work in planning ingenious jokes and tricks. She quickly became popular with the third form, for she was sunny-natured and shared June's mischievous sense of fun. But she was not quite as bold and daring as June, nor did she have the hardness and malice that were such flaws in the other girl's character.

'I like her tremendously,' said Susan to Felicity one day, as the two of them chatted about the new girls. 'I just hope that June's don't-care-ishness doesn't rub off on her.'

'Perhaps Freddie's good-heartedness will rub off on June,' suggested Felicity. 'I must say, she's the only one of the three new girls that I'm really keen on.'

Certainly Amy was far too stuck-up to be popular, while the teachers found her extremely trying as well, for her work was far below the standard of most of the form.

'I can't decide whether she's lazy, or stupid, or both!' an exasperated Miss Peters said to Miss Potts in the mistresses' common-room, after she had struggled to mark one of Amy's essays. 'She doesn't seem to understand the basic rules of grammar, she's hopeless at maths, not the slightest bit interested in history, and – according to Miss Maxwell – won't exert herself at all when it comes to games and swimming, for she doesn't like getting red-faced and untidy! The only thing Amy is any good at is French.'

Having spent so many holidays in France, Amy did, indeed, speak the language very well, which pleased both Mam'zelles enormously.

Bonnie was not much better than Amy at lessons but, having spent most of her time with adults, she had become extremely clever at 'twisting them around her little finger', as a disgruntled Nora put it. Poor Nora had had her nose pushed very much out of joint by Bonnie's arrival. She had always taken for granted that she was Mam'zelle Dupont's favourite, making a joke of it and using her position to advantage when it suited her. But now she found that she didn't like to see another girl taking her place. Mam'zelle Dupont positively doted on Bonnie, although her French was poor, while Miss Simmons, the quiet little needlework teacher, was thrilled to find a member of the third form who could sew well. Miss Linnie, the art mistress, and Mr Young, the singing teacher, were also charmed by Bonnie, and gave her a very easy time indeed.

But not all of the teachers were fond of Bonnie. The blunt, downright Miss Peters considered her an empty-headed little creature, with far too many airs and graces, while Mam'zelle Rougier, who made it a habit to dislike those girls who were favoured by Mam'zelle Dupont, remained unmoved by either Bonnie's tears or her smiles.

As for Miss Maxwell, the games mistress, she was driven to distraction by the girl.

Bonnie had never been swimming in her life, and her shrill squeal as she entered the cold water for the first time made everyone jump, including Miss Maxwell.

'Bonnie!' she said angrily. 'I thought that you were in difficulties, judging from the noise you're making, but the water is barely up to your waist!'

Then Susan swam past and accidentally splashed water in Bonnie's face, which caused her to scream again.

'Baby!' said June scornfully to Felicity. 'Honestly, anyone would think that Susan was trying to drown her. I've a good mind to duck her – at least then she wouldn't be able to scream!'

Felicity grinned, but the smile was wiped off her face a few moments later when, as she was poised to dive into the pool, Bonnie let out an ear-splitting yell, because Veronica – whether deliberately, or by accident, nobody was sure – barged into her and almost knocked her over. Distracted, Felicity lost her balance, and instead of swallow-diving gracefully into the pool she did an undignified belly-flop and almost landed on top of a very surprised Pam!

'I have had quite enough of this!' said Miss Maxwell, losing her temper. 'Bonnie, I really can't allow you to disrupt the third form's swimming like this any longer. Please get out of the pool at once and get dressed!'

'Yes, Miss Maxwell,' said Bonnie meekly, hurrying to climb out of the pool.

Only Felicity caught the tiny little smile on the girl's face just before she turned to walk back up to the school, and she gave a gasp.

'The little monkey!' Felicity thought to herself. 'I believe that Bonnie played up deliberately to get out of swimming!'

But, as much as she exasperated the others, Bonnie did have her good points. She was extremely loyal to those she considered her friends, as Veronica found out when she made the mistake of criticising Felicity to Amy in front of her.

'I can't *think* what made Miss Peters choose Felicity Rivers as head-girl,' Veronica said, in a sneering tone. 'I don't think she's a good leader at all, for her character is far too weak. If you ask me, she only got the position because her sister was Head Girl last year.'

Amy opened her mouth to reply, but before she could speak, a furious Bonnie confronted Veronica, saying angrily, 'You take that back at once! How dare you say things like that about Felicity? I think that she's a jolly good head-girl, and she's my friend, and I won't have you making spiteful remarks about her!'

Both Veronica and Amy were quite taken aback, and since Veronica – who preferred to make her criticisms behind people's backs rather than to their faces – didn't want her remarks getting back to Felicity, she did not retaliate.

But Julie, who had been sitting nearby, had overheard the whole conversation, and had, in fact, been about to leap to Felicity's defence when Bonnie stepped in, and the new girl at once went up in her estimation.

Bonnie's loyalty came to the fore again a few days later, in the French lesson – and this time she surprised the whole form!

Mam'zelle Dupont was not in the best of tempers, for the first form, who she had just left, had played her up quite dreadfully. Which was unfortunate for June, who – feeling a little bored – had also chosen that morning to act the goat.

Lifting the lid of her desk to hide from Mam'zelle's view, she ripped a page from her exercise book and swiftly folded it into a paper aeroplane.

'Freddie,' she whispered. 'I bet I can hit the back of Amy's head from here.'

'And I bet you can't!' answered Freddie at once, with a grin. 'She's too far away.'

Bonnie, who sat across the aisle from the two girls, didn't hear this exchange, but she caught the sudden movement as June raised her hand and launched her paper aeroplane on its journey. Mam'zelle, who had turned her back to the class while she wrote something on the blackboard, remained in blissful ignorance, until a few giggles broke out as the aeroplane glided gracefully over Amy's head and, much to her surprise, landed on her desk. Amy picked the aeroplane up and Mam'zelle, who had whipped round upon hearing the giggles, glared at her furiously.

'So!' she said angrily. 'You are so good at French that you can waste the class's time in this way, Amy?'

Poor Amy looked horrified and protested, 'But Mam'zelle, I didn't throw the aeroplane! I was just –'

'Be silent!' cried Mam'zelle, her black eyes snapping coldly. 'How dare you interrupt me? You are a bad and disrespectful girl, Amy, and you will be punished. Tonight you will learn the whole of the French poem we have just started, and you will say it back to me tomorrow.'

Amy, stung by the injustice of this, longed to argue but didn't dare. When Mam'zelle was in this sort of mood, she was quite likely to make her learn *two* poems! Why didn't the mean beast who had thrown the aeroplane own up and get her out of trouble? In fact June, at the back of the class, was about to do just that. She might have her faults, but she wasn't about to allow someone else to be punished for her joke. Before she could do so, however, Bonnie got to her feet and piped up, 'Mam'zelle! It wasn't Amy who threw the aeroplane – it was June. I saw her.'

The third formers, who had very strict ideas about telling tales, gasped, looking at one another in horror, and at Bonnie in disgust. Felicity gave a groan. Of course, never having been to school before, Bonnie probably didn't realise that it wasn't done to tell on one's form-mates. And, as head-girl, it was up to Felicity to put her straight!

'June, is this true?' said Mam'zelle, looking sternly at the girl. 'And you did not have the courage to tell the truth, even when *la pauvre* Amy was about to be punished?'

'It's true that I threw the plane, Mam'zelle,' said June, going very red as she stood up. 'But I was about to own up, truly I was.'

'I don't believe you!' cried Amy, who disliked June intensely and felt very grateful to Bonnie for coming to her rescue. 'You probably did it on purpose to get me into trouble.'

'I did not!' said June indignantly. 'It was just a joke, but –'

'Enough!' shouted Mam'zelle, stamping one of her little feet crossly. 'June, *méchante fille*, you will have the punishment that I was going to give the poor, innocent Amy. You will learn that poem, and you will recite it to me tomorrow. And, as a second punishment for not owning up, you will go to bed half an hour early this evening!'

The girl was horrified, and smarted at the injustice of the second punishment. But, bold as she was, even June did not dare to argue with an angry Mam'zelle Dupont, so she said meekly, 'Yes, Mam'zelle,' and took her seat again. But she glared angrily at Bonnie, and Felicity, turning in her seat to give June a sympathetic look, saw it. 'Oh dear,' she thought. 'There's going to be trouble!'

And Felicity was quite right, for June marched up to her at break-time, a stormy expression on her face as she said, 'I say, Felicity, what are we going to do about Bonnie? She simply can't be allowed to get away with sneaking like that.'

'No, I suppose you're right and something will have to be done about her,' said Felicity. 'There's no time now, but we'll hold a form meeting in the common-room at lunchtime.'

So as soon as lunch was over, the members of the third

form trooped into the common-room. Only one person was missing, and that was Bonnie.

'Where is she?' demanded June, her eyes flashing angrily. 'I suppose the little coward doesn't have the courage to face me.'

'Actually, June, Miss Peters wanted to see Bonnie about some prep,' said Amy coldly. 'She'll be here shortly.'

Felicity, who didn't want to be too hard on Bonnie, was quite glad that the girl wasn't there yet, and she clapped her hands together for silence, before saying, 'June, I quite understand that you're angry, but please let's not forget that Bonnie hasn't been to school before and doesn't quite understand all our ways.'

'Oh, you would stick up for her, Felicity!' said June, a harsh note in her voice. 'Just wait until the little sneak shows her face! My word, won't I tell her what I think of her! The silly baby is always turning on the waterworks over something or other – and this time I'll give her something to cry about!'

This was exactly what Felicity was afraid of. June in a rage was not a pleasant sight, and little Bonnie would never be able to stand up to her.

'No, June!' said Felicity firmly. 'I am head-girl, and I am running this meeting, and Bonnie will be given a chance to have her say. Then the form as a whole will decide if she is to be punished, and how.'

Just then the door opened and Bonnie herself entered. Felicity moved forward to speak to her, but June got in first. Throwing Felicity a mocking look, she stalked up to

Bonnie and said menacingly, 'What do you mean by sneaking on me to Mam'zelle Dupont, you horrid little beast?'

The third formers watched with bated breath, some of them hoping that Bonnie would get what she deserved, others hoping that June would not go too far, and *all* of them waiting for Bonnie to burst into noisy tears. A worried expression on her face, Felicity braced herself, ready to step in if the need arose.

But June had underestimated the new girl. Bonnie wasn't used to being spoken to in such a way, and she didn't like it one little bit. She didn't much like June either, and was quite shrewd enough to realise that tears would not work with her. So she met the girl's angry gaze squarely and said coldly, 'Don't be ridiculous. I did nothing of the sort.'

June gave an outraged gasp. 'So you're a liar, Bonnie, as well as a sneak! The whole form heard you tell Mam'zelle that it was I who threw that paper aeroplane.'

There were murmurs of agreement from the listening girls, but Bonnie said quite calmly, 'Yes, that's right. Amy was going to be punished for something you had done, so I stepped in and told Mam'zelle the truth. But I did *not* sneak! You see, my dear June, sneaking means just that. It means going behind someone's back, doing something sly and secretive and underhand. I spoke up in front of the whole form, so I really don't see how there was anything sneaky about it!'

Felicity stared at the girl in surprise, for what Bonnie

had said was quite true – she *had* told tales, but she had been perfectly open about it.

June swiftly recovered and said, 'Very well, perhaps "sneak" is the wrong word in this case, but you *did* tell on me!'

'Yes, to get a friend out of trouble,' retorted Bonnie, just as quickly. 'And I must say, June, I would have thought better of you if you had owned up yourself.'

There was just enough scorn in the girl's tone to throw June on the defensive and she said hotly, 'I *was* going to own up, as I tried to explain to Mam'zelle! But I didn't get the chance, thanks to you!'

'Well, how was I to know that?' said Bonnie, opening her eyes wide. 'I'm the new girl, don't forget. I don't know anything about your character, June – whether you're the kind of person who will keep quiet and let someone else take her punishment, or the kind of person who will come clean and take the consequences.'

'I'm no coward!' said June indignantly. 'I would never let anyone else take the blame for something I had done.'

'I'm very glad to hear it,' said Bonnie with a little smile. 'It's just a pity that you weren't a bit quicker in taking the blame, then all of this unpleasantness could have been avoided. I hope that this will be a lesson to you, June. Now, if you'll excuse me, I need to go and speak to Matron.'

And with that, Bonnie swept from the room with her little head held high, leaving behind her a stunned silence. Susan, who was doing her best not to smile, nudged Felicity and nodded towards June, still standing in the middle of the floor, with her mouth open like a goldfish. Felicity bit her lip hard to stop herself from laughing. Pam and Julie, meanwhile, were clinging to one another as they tried to stifle their laughter, while Nora's shoulders shook uncontrollably with mirth. Even Veronica, jealous as she was of Bonnie, had relished seeing June rendered speechless, while Amy had enjoyed the scene tremendously.

Suddenly, a loud burst of laughter broke the silence, and the girls were amazed to realise that it came from June herself!

'My goodness!' she gasped, when she was able to speak. 'Who would have thought that little scrap would be able to stand up to me like that? But she did, and I must say that I admire her for it!'

And the third formers, joining in June's laughter, admired *her* for being able to admit so honestly that someone had got the better of her. You could always rely on June to do the unexpected, thought Felicity wryly, feeling quite relieved that the row was over. But, when she thought about it later, she felt a little uneasy. June had flouted her authority by refusing to allow her, Felicity, to run the meeting her way, and by confronting Bonnie when she had been told not to. And Felicity, anxious to avoid a row, had allowed her to get away with it. What would Darrell have done in that situation, she wondered? The answer to that was easy, for Darrell was such a frank, forthright person that she would have had no hesitation at all in putting June in her place. Well, if June continued to flout her, Felicity would have to find the strength of character to deal with her in the same way. After all, she was head-girl, and the third formers needed someone strong to lead them, and set an example, not someone who shrank from difficult or unpleasant tasks. Felicity made a promise to herself, there and then. It wouldn't be easy, and no doubt she would make mistakes along the way, but she *would* become a strong leader.

A dirty trick

June felt sore with Mam'zelle Dupont for some time after the 'aeroplane affair', as it became known. She had felt extremely humiliated at going to bed half an hour before the others, and, the next morning, had recited the French poem to the mistress in a sulky tone. Mam'zelle, who had begun to feel a little sorry that she had been so hard on the girl, noticed the tone, and June's petulant expression, and hardened her heart. Ah, she was a bad girl, this June, and a little punishment would be good for her.

Freddie, who admired June tremendously, also felt angry on her friend's behalf, and wished that she could think of some way of getting back at Mam'zelle Dupont.

Then June came up to Freddie one break-time and, taking her arm, said, 'I'm bored. Nothing ever happens around here! I think it's time we played the magic soap trick on Amy.'

'Super!' giggled Freddie. 'Shall we let the others in on it?'

June thought for a moment, then said, 'No, let's plan it out between ourselves – just the two of us! Then we can surprise the others.'

Freddie nodded happily and said, 'But how can we be

certain that Amy will use the right soap? If she doesn't it will simply ruin the whole trick.'

'I've thought of that,' said June with a grin. 'Amy has a bar of very expensive soap that her mother sent her, and it looks very like our special soap, so I'm simply going to switch the bars. She'll never notice the difference, and there's no fear of anyone else getting a dirty face, because dear Amy would *never* let anyone else use her precious soap!'

Freddie chuckled. 'Oh, June, it's going to be simply marvellous! And the whole of North Tower will be able to share in the fun, because Amy's face should start to turn muddy at breakfast-time. When are we going to do it?'

'Tomorrow,' answered June. 'I noticed this morning that Amy has almost used up all of her old bar of soap, which means that she will open the new one tomorrow.'

Freddie said nothing, for an idea had just come to her – an idea so breathtakingly bold and daring that June herself might have come up with it. But Freddie decided to say nothing to June, for she was going to give her friend a surprise. And she was going to give the whole of North Tower the biggest laugh it had ever had!

Felicity wondered what June and Freddie were up to as the third form dressed the following morning. The two of them whispered together excitedly, and there was a very mischievous twinkle in Freddie's eye! Freddie had asked June if she could switch the soap bars, and June had agreed. 'Be careful, though,' she had warned. 'Make sure that no one's around when you do it, and see that you put our special soap in exactly the same place as Amy's soap was. We don't want her smelling a rat!'

Now the two girls nudged one another and giggled as they watched Amy take the soap from the drawer of her cabinet and walk into the bathroom.

'What *are* you two up to?' asked Felicity, unable to contain her curiosity any longer.

'Why, nothing at all, Felicity,' answered June, making her expression as innocent as she possibly could. 'What makes you think that we're up to something?'

'You both seem very excited about something,' said Felicity, eyeing them suspiciously. 'Come on – come clean!'

Freddie gave a sudden snort of laughter, and June's lips twitched as she said, 'But there's nothing to come clean about, Felicity. Really there isn't. We're not trying to soft-soap you.'

This was too much for Freddie, who collapsed on to her bed in a fit of giggles and Felicity, realising that she wasn't going to get anything out of the pair, shook her head and went off to join Susan.

June gave Amy a sidelong glance as she came out of the bathroom, but the magic soap had not begun to do its work yet, and her complexion looked as clean and fresh as ever. But it wouldn't stay that way for long, thought June, smiling to herself. Just you wait, Amy!

But, as breakfast wore on, and Amy's face stayed the same, June grew impatient.

'Why is nothing happening?' she muttered under her

breath to Freddie. 'Don't say that Alicia has given me a dud bar of soap!'

'I'm sure she hasn't,' said Freddie confidently. 'In fact, I think that things are just about to happen!'

June lifted her head sharply, then realised that Freddie wasn't looking at Amy, but at the head of the table, where Mam'zelle Dupont sat. She followed Freddie's gaze – and gave a gasp! For Mam'zelle's skin was turning a muddy, dingy brown.

Pam and Susan, who sat either side of the French mistress, couldn't fail to notice the startling transformation as well, and they stared at Mam'zelle, who was quite unaware of her strange appearance, in mingled horror and astonishment. Each of them nudged the girl next to her, and soon the word was passed around the table, and the third form were all gazing at Mam'zelle, trying desperately to control their laughter. Most of the girls guessed, of course, that June had played a trick using the soap that Alicia had given her, but they simply couldn't imagine how she had got Mam'zelle to use it. How clever of her!

June couldn't imagine how Mam'zelle had got hold of the magic soap either, and turned to Freddie, but before she could ask for an explanation, a cry came from the head of the table. Mam'zelle had just looked down at her hands, and realised that they were covered in dirty, muddy streaks.

'*Mon dieu!*' she exclaimed. 'My hands, they are filthy. Yet I washed them this morning. What can have caused this?'

Carefully she examined her cup, her plate and even her

knife and fork, for dirty marks, and this was too much for Nora, who gave one of her sudden snorts of laughter. Most of the others were having difficulty in controlling their mirth as well, and people at the other tables began to notice.

'My word, just look at Mam'zelle Dupont!'

'What*ever* has happened to her?'

'Has she forgotten to have a wash this morning?'

'It must be a trick! I'll bet it was June!'

Mam'zelle became aware of the whispering and looked most uncomfortable, and Felicity took pity on her.

'Mam'zelle,' she said, when she could trust her voice enough to speak. 'I'm afraid it's not just your hands that are dirty, but your face as well.'

Amy, who always carried a little mirror around with her, fished it out of her pocket and handed it to the French mistress, who took one look at her reflection and gave a piercing shriek.

The dining-room was in uproar by this time and the other mistresses, who had now had a good look at Mam'zelle's dirty face, stared at one another in consternation. Miss Potts took charge, getting to her feet and raising her voice to demand silence.

'That will do!' she commanded. 'Mam'zelle Dupont, I don't understand how you appear to be covered in mud, since you looked quite clean when you first came in to breakfast, but I suggest that you go to one of the bathrooms and wash it off before your first class begins.'

So, summoning up what dignity she could, the little

French mistress tottered from the dining-room, and Miss Potts said sharply, 'June! I don't suppose you know anything about this, do you?'

'No, I don't, Miss Potts,' answered June quite truthfully, and Miss Potts stared at her hard, knowing that she could play the innocent very well when it suited her. But the girl looked just as bewildered as the others, though she didn't seem to find it as funny as they did – in fact, she looked rather angry.

'Well, it's a mystery to me how Mam'zelle Dupont could have entered the room looking as neat as a new pin, and left it looking as though she had been in a mud fight!' said Miss Potts. 'I don't know if I shall ever get to the bottom of it. Now, girls, please finish your breakfast quietly, then make your way to your first lesson.'

Miss Potts went back to the first-form table and, as soon as she was out of earshot, a babble of low-voiced chatter broke out among the third formers.

'June! It was you, wasn't it?'

'Of course it was. You used the magic soap on Mam'zelle, didn't you?'

'I must say, it was a splendid trick! Did you see poor old Mam'zelle's face?'

'Just like you not to own up.'

This last remark came from Amy, and June replied, 'I didn't own up because it wasn't me who played the trick, I tell you!'

'Then who was it?' asked Felicity, puzzled.

'It was me!' said Freddie gleefully, her eyes alight with

79

mischief. 'I did it to get back at Mam'zelle for being so hard on June the other day.'

Pam chuckled. 'Well, you certainly did that all right! So, do you mean to say that June wasn't in on the trick at all?'

'No,' said June rather shortly. 'I *thought* that I was, but it seems that Freddie decided to go it alone and use the soap on Mam'zelle, instead of the person we had chosen.'

'You'd better watch your step, June,' laughed Nora. 'Freddie will be taking over from you as the form joker if you aren't careful.'

June said nothing, and Freddie stared at her, rather puzzled at her coolness. Anyone would think that she wasn't happy about getting her revenge on Mam'zelle Dupont.

In fact, June was simply furious with Freddie for stealing her thunder. *She* was the leader in their friendship, and she wouldn't have it any other way. She was quite happy for Freddie to play second fiddle to her, and to act as her assistant in planning jokes and tricks, but she, June, was the joker of the form and no one was going to take that position away from her. Where another girl might have taken pleasure in getting top marks in class, or for her sporting achievements, all June cared about was getting praise for her jokes and tricks. And she didn't like to see Freddie getting a share of that praise now, feeling extremely jealous as the others congratulated her.

'Simply marvellous, Freddie,' said Susan, clapping her on the back. 'But however did you get Mam'zelle to use the soap?'

'Oh, it was easy, really,' answered Freddie. 'I just slipped into her bathroom when I knew that she was taking prep with the second form, and left the soap there.'

'Heavens, how daring!' said Bonnie, her eyes wide with admiration. 'What if someone had seen you?'

'Thank goodness no one did!' said Julie. 'That was the best laugh I've had in simply ages.'

June pushed her bowl of half-eaten porridge away, her appetite completely gone and her thoughts racing. Much as she liked the girl, Freddie was going to have to learn that there was only room for one joker in the third form. June would have to think of a way to turn Freddie's thoughts and energies in another direction. But how?

The answer came to June, quite by chance, one Saturday morning. She walked into the cloakroom to find Felicity and Susan putting on their hats and coats and said, 'Hallo – where are you two off to?'

'Oh, we thought we'd just go for a walk in the countryside,' answered Felicity. 'It's gloriously sunny out, although it's a little chilly.'

'Julie's ridden Jack over to Bill and Clarissa's,' put in Susan. 'And Nora and Pam have gone with her, so we thought we might make our way over there too.'

Bill and Clarissa were two old girls who had been in the same form as Darrell and Alicia, and they now ran a riding stables not far from the school. The Malory Towers girls were very fond of Bill and Clarissa, and often visited them, either to go riding or just for a chat. Miss Peters, who was also a great horse-woman and a close friend of the pair, was a regular visitor too.

'I say, do you mind if I tag along?' asked June. 'Poor old Freddie's been giving a basketful of mending to do by Matron and it's going to take her simply ages, so I'm at a bit of a loose end.'

So June put her hat and coat on, and soon the three girls were striding out of the gates of Malory Towers and along a pretty country lane, carpeted with russet autumn leaves.

'My word, this wind is pretty blustery,' said Susan, holding her hat on her head. 'Thank goodness we're not walking along the cliff, or we should have been blown over.'

Suddenly June stopped dead and lifted her finger, saying, 'Hush a minute! I think I heard something.'

The other two fell silent, then they heard the noise too – a plaintive little mew. This was followed by a woman's voice, saying, 'Oh dear, Sooty, don't say you've got stuck in that apple tree again! Now, how on earth am I to get you down?'

'It's coming from the garden of that little cottage over there,' said Felicity. 'I think that we should see if we can help.'

The cottage was surrounded by a wall, with a wooden gate in the middle, and the three girls let themselves in, to see an elderly lady standing in the middle of a neat little garden, looking up at an apple tree with an expression of dismay.

'Excuse me,' said Felicity. 'It sounds as if you're in some sort of trouble and we came to see if we could help.'

'Oh, how kind,' said the lady, her worried face creasing into a smile as she turned to face the three girls. 'Do you see what has happened? That silly cat of mine has been climbing the apple tree, and now he's got himself stuck and can't get down. Sooty doesn't seem to realise that I'm not as young as I used to be and can't go climbing up after him any more!'

The pitiful mew sounded again, this time from above their heads, and the girls looked up to see a little pointed black face with brilliant green eyes staring down at them.

'Don't worry,' said June, stepping towards the tree. 'I'll have Sooty down in a trice.'

Quickly and agilely she began to climb, while Felicity stood at the bottom of the tree ready to take the cat from her. Susan, meanwhile, chatted to the old lady, whose name was Mrs Dale.

'Do be careful, dear!' Mrs Dale called out, as June climbed ever higher. 'I'd never forgive myself if you were to fall and hurt yourself.'

But June had been climbing trees since she could walk, and this one presented no problem to her. Soon she reached the branch the frightened Sooty was on, and she grabbed him firmly, tucking him into the front of her coat to keep him secure, before shinning back down again. Sooty wasn't too pleased about being handed over to Felicity, and dug his claws firmly into June's coat, but the two girls managed to dislodge him and Felicity placed him safely on the ground.

'How can I ever thank you?' said Mrs Dale, stooping to stroke the little black cat.

'All in a day's work,' said June breezily. 'And now, I suppose, we'd best be on our way.'

'Oh no, you must come in and have some homemade cake and lemonade,' insisted Mrs Dale. 'It's the least I can do after you've rescued my Sooty. Besides, I don't get many visitors and I should enjoy your company.'

So, within minutes, the girls were seated round the table in Mrs Dale's cosy kitchen, enjoying big slices of the most delicious fruit cake, washed down with lemonade.

'This cake is first rate, Mrs Dale,' said Susan.

'Well, it's nice to see you girls enjoying it,' said the old lady, smiling. 'I suppose you all come from Malory Towers?'

'That's right,' said Felicity.

'Well, you're a credit to the school. Actually, my granddaughter goes there. I wonder if you know her? Her name is Amy Ryder-Cochrane.'

The three girls almost choked on their lemonade, for they would never have imagined that Mrs Dale was related to the snobbish Amy. Mrs Dale was just a nice, ordinary old lady, very like their own grandmothers, and there was nothing grand about her at all, while the little cottage she lived in was very modest indeed. The girls exchanged startled glances and Felicity said, 'Yes, we know Amy. She's in the same form as us.'

'But she never mentioned that she had a grandmother living nearby,' said June.

'Ah well, she wouldn't,' said Mrs Dale. 'Because she doesn't know I'm here.'

The old lady became pensive, looking at the girls as though deciding whether or not she could trust them. Eventually, it seemed, she decided that she could, for she went on, 'You see, my dears, Amy's father is a very wealthy, well-connected gentleman. And when he married my daughter, he didn't want all his fancy friends and relatives knowing that she came from quite a common background, so she wasn't allowed to see very much of me.'

The girls listened, appalled, and Felicity murmured to Susan, 'Now we can see where Amy gets her snobbishness from.'

'And when Amy was born, he didn't want her having anything to do with me either,' said Mrs Dale. 'My daughter brought her to see me when she was a baby, but I haven't seen her since. Jane – that's my daughter – visits now and again, but she never brings Amy because that husband of hers wouldn't approve.'

The girls didn't know quite what to say. Mrs Dale sounded quite matter-of-fact about the whole situation, but there was a hint of sadness in the faded blue eyes. It was left to the outspoken June to say what they were all thinking. 'But that's absolutely dreadful!' she burst out. 'Don't worry, Mrs Dale, we'll tell Amy that you're here and bring her along to visit you.'

'Oh no, my dear, you mustn't!' said the old lady, looking quite alarmed. 'You see, whatever my feelings are, it wouldn't be right to encourage her to disobey her father.

I admit that when I learned she was coming to school here, I hoped that I might get a glimpse of her now and then, for all I have of her is a photo that was taken when she was about five years old. But it would be very wrong of me to ask her to go behind her father's back, so I must ask you all not to betray my confidence.'

Rather reluctantly, the three girls promised Mrs Dale that they wouldn't divulge to Amy that she was living near the school, and the old lady seemed happy with this.

The girls, though, were far from happy, and they discussed the matter as they went on their way to the riding stables.

'Amy's father must be a dreadful man,' said Susan, giving a shudder.

'Well, her mother must be pretty awful too, for agreeing to turn her back on her own mother!' said June. 'My goodness, if *my* father tried to tell Mother that she couldn't take me to visit my granny she would soon tell him where to get off!'

'Yes, so would mine,' said Felicity. She gave a sigh. 'It's such a pity that we can't let on to Amy. Mrs Dale seems such a nice woman, and she's awfully lonely. I daresay a few visits from Amy would cheer her up no end.'

'Yes,' said June, looking thoughtful. 'Yes, I expect they would.'

Felicity, who mistrusted June when she wore that thoughtful expression, said sharply, 'Now listen, June! I don't know what's in your mind, but we gave our word to

Mrs Dale that we wouldn't say anything to Amy, and we must keep it.'

'My dear Felicity, I have no intention of saying anything to Amy,' said June.

'Good,' said Felicity. 'And we'd better not mention it to any of the others, either. We'll just keep it a secret between the three of us.'

Secrets and tricks

But June did tell someone else about Amy's grandmother – she told Freddie.

'You must promise not to say a word to any of the others, though,' June warned her solemnly. 'And don't let on that I've told you, or Felicity won't be very pleased.'

'I shan't say a word, June,' said Freddie, who had listened open-mouthed to June's tale. 'You can count on me. It's quite a sad story, isn't it? Poor Mrs Dale!'

'She's such a dear old lady,' said June, with a sigh. 'And I felt so sorry for her, for she seems awfully lonely. I did think of an idea to help her, but . . .'

June's voice tailed off and Freddie prompted eagerly, 'But what? Do tell, June.'

June sighed again and said, 'There's no point, for it wouldn't work. It needs someone really bold and daring to carry it off, and I just can't think of anyone who could do it.'

Freddie laughed. 'But there's no one bolder or more daring than you, June! Why can't *you* carry out this mysterious idea yourself?'

'Because Mrs Dale has already met me,' answered June. 'Besides, my colouring is too different from Amy's.'

Freddie's brow wrinkled in puzzlement. 'But what does your colouring have to do with anything? June, you simply must tell me what you have in mind, or I shall die of curiosity.'

'All right then,' said June. 'You see, Freddie, we can't break our word and tell Amy about her grandmother. So I thought it would be rather a splendid idea if we could get someone else to pretend to be Amy, and go and visit the old lady now and again, to cheer her up.'

Freddie gave a low whistle. 'We'd never get away with it! Mrs Dale would know at once that the impostor wasn't Amy.'

'No, she wouldn't,' said June. 'She hasn't seen Amy since she was a baby, and the only photograph she has of her is one that was taken when she was five. All we would need to do is choose someone fair – like you, or Nora.'

Freddie digested this for a moment, then said, 'Felicity would go mad if she found out.'

June gave a rather mocking little laugh. 'Oh, Felicity can be dreadfully pi at times. Not that there's any reason why she *should* find out.' She pretended to think for a moment, then went on, 'I wonder if Nora could be persuaded? It means letting someone else in on the secret, but that can't be helped. She might be a little scatter-brained, but she's good-hearted and I think she would want to help Mrs Dale. Nora's a good actress, and pretty daring, too – I don't think that *she* would be frightened of upsetting Felicity!'

June's tone was slightly scornful, and Freddie was

stung. She looked up to the other girl no end, and badly wanted to impress her. Lifting her chin, she said, 'There's no need to involve Nora, June. I'll do it!'

'Are you sure?' asked June, looking hard at her friend.

'Absolutely positive,' answered Freddie firmly. 'Look, there's half an hour until bedtime – let's slip away to the little music room near the dormy. No one ever uses it, so we shall be able to make some plans without being interrupted.'

So the girls made their plans, and, by the following Saturday afternoon, they were ready to put them into action. Freddie was full of bravado as she and June made their way along the lane to Mrs Dale's, keeping up a stream of light-hearted chatter. Inwardly, though, she felt extremely nervous and was even beginning to wish that she had never allowed June to talk her into this. But June – well aware of Freddie's nerves – kept going on about how happy the old lady would be, and how no one else but Freddie would be able to pull this off successfully, and looked at her with such admiration that it was impossible to back out. Within moments, it seemed to Freddie, they were knocking on Mrs Dale's door. The old lady opened it, giving a little start of surprise as she saw June. 'Why, it's the girl who rescued my cat!' she said. 'How nice to see you again, dear. And you've brought a friend! Do come in, both of you.'

She ushered the two girls into the kitchen, and June took Freddie – who was doing her utmost to remain in the background – by the arm, pulling her forward. 'I have a surprise for you, Mrs Dale,' she said, launching into the little speech that she had rehearsed. 'I know that you didn't want me and the others to tell Amy that you were here, and we kept our word. But I'm afraid that the three of us discussed the matter in the common-room later, and – unknown to us – Amy was outside, and she overheard us.'

Mrs Dale put her hand up to her mouth, an expression of dismay on her face. 'So she knows that I'm here?' she said. 'My Amy knows?'

Now it was Freddie's turn to speak, but her vocal chords seemed to have become paralysed. Unseen by Mrs Dale, June prodded her sharply in the back and, rather hoarsely, Freddie said, 'Yes, Gran. I know. And I insisted that June brought me to meet you.'

'Amy?' said Mrs Dale, her pale blue eyes opening wide. 'Amy, is it really you?'

Freddie nodded and June, smiling to herself in quiet satisfaction, said softly, 'I'm sure that the two of you must have a lot to talk about, so I'll go and leave you to it. Amy, I'll see you back at school in time for tea. Don't be late!'

Mrs Dale, still looking hard at Freddie, didn't seem to hear June, but Freddie did and stared at her in horror. This wasn't part of the plan! June had promised that she would stay and that she, Freddie, would not be left alone with Mrs Dale.

'June, wait!' she cried. But it was too late – June was already out of the door, and Mrs Dale was telling Freddie to sit herself down and she would make them both a nice cup of tea. Freddie had no choice but to do as she was told, though inwardly she was seething. Just wait until she caught up with June later!

June, for her part, was extremely pleased with herself and whistled jauntily as she made her way back to the school. Everything had gone just as she had hoped! Of course, Freddie would be simply furious with her, but June excelled at talking herself out of trouble and she would soon smooth things over.

But when the two girls met up outside the dining-room just before tea, Freddie seemed to have got over her ill temper. In fact, much to her own surprise, she had had an absolutely splendid time at Mrs Dale's! Freddie had no grandmother of her own, for both of hers had died when she was little, and she had often felt envious of other girls when they talked about their own devoted grandmothers, and how they spoiled them. So spending time with Mrs Dale had been a novel experience for the girl, and a very enjoyable one. Once Freddie had got over her nerves a little, the two of them had got along like a house on fire. Of course, Freddie hadn't been able to relax completely, for she had to guard her tongue so that she didn't give the game away. Even so, she had been delighted when Mrs Dale invited her to tea the following day.

'I know it's not what your father would like,' the old lady had said. 'I didn't set out to make you go against his wishes, but it's done now. We've met and there's nothing he can do about it. All the same, though, I don't think you should mention it to him just yet. Or your mother, for that matter.'

Freddie related all of this to June in a low voice as they had their tea, and June listened intently, pleased when the girl said that she was going to Mrs Dale's again tomorrow. The more the two saw of one another, the better, as far as June was concerned. Ah, Freddie might be enjoying herself now, but it wouldn't be long before her conscience began to prick her.

Meanwhile, June had a plan of her own to carry out – one that Freddie did not play a part in. Ever since Freddie had tricked Mam'zelle with the magic soap, June had been trying to think up a trick of her own – and this time she was determined that the glory would be hers and hers alone. And now she had come up with something which would put Freddie's effort in the shade. The victim, yet again, was to be poor, unsuspecting Mam'zelle Dupont, of course, and June smiled to herself as she pictured the reaction that her trick would get.

At the back of the third form's classroom, right behind June's seat, was a door into a small storage room. The room was home to old books, long-lost property and all kinds of odds and ends that nobody really wanted, and it was kept permanently locked. But June had discovered that the key hung on a nail in the handyman's little cubby-hole and, her ingenious brain getting to work, she had come up with a first-rate plan for baffling Mam'zelle.

That evening, as the third formers prepared for bed, Amy picked up a pot of cream from her cabinet and removed the lid. The girl was extremely vain about her complexion and possessed a marvellous array of lotions and potions. She was forever smearing something or other on to her face and the others often teased her about it.

'What do all these creams actually *do*, Amy?' asked Felicity, watching her in fascination.

'This one is a vanishing cream,' answered Amy, peering into the mirror.

'Well, it doesn't work,' called out June. 'We can still see you!'

'Oh, very funny, June,' said Amy. 'Actually, it's supposed to make spots and blemishes vanish. And now I've just used the last of it, so I'll have to ask Mummy to send me some more.'

She threw the empty pot into the wastepaper basket, and June gazed at it thoughtfully for a moment. Then she went and retrieved it from the basket, asking, 'Amy, is it all right if I have this?'

'If you really want an empty pot,' answered Amy, looking surprised. 'Though I can't imagine what use you have for it.'

'Oh, I have a use for it all right,' said June, grinning. 'Just you wait and see!'

June decided to play her trick on Monday morning, and took the others into her confidence the night before, when they were all gathered in the common-room. The third formers listened raptly as June explained what she intended to do, their eyes lighting up and broad grins on their faces. Even Veronica was looking forward to it, for she was no scholar, particularly when it came to French, and always felt in low spirits on Monday mornings, with the weekend over and a whole week of lessons ahead of her. Strangely enough, the only person who didn't seem thrilled at the idea was Freddie, who was unusually quiet and pre-occupied.

'Anything wrong, old girl?' Felicity asked in concern, noticing that the girl didn't seem her usual self.

'Mm? Oh, no, everything's fine, Felicity,' answered Freddie rather distractedly. 'I'm just a little tired, that's all.'

'Of course, you were out in the fresh air all afternoon, weren't you?' said Susan. 'Where did you get to?'

June quickly shot Freddie a warning glance, but it was quite unnecessary. She had no intention of saying anything that might alert the others to the fact that she had been to Mrs Dale's. Instead she replied vaguely, 'Oh, I just took a long walk along the coast road and the sea air has really made me feel sleepy.'

Felicity looked at her closely and frowned. Freddie didn't look tired – she looked as if she was worried about something. June was watching her friend too – but she knew exactly what was bothering her! Freddie had hardly touched a thing at teatime. Of course, that could have been because she had already eaten at Mrs Dale's earlier, but it didn't explain her rather subdued air. June had managed to snatch a few minutes alone with Freddie before prep and the girl said in a worried tone, 'June, I really didn't think this through properly when I agreed to pretend to be Amy. How am I going to get out of it? I can't go *on* pretending to be her all the time I'm at Malory Towers.'

'It's easy enough,' said June with a careless shrug. 'Just keep it up for a little while longer, then you can pretend that your parents – or rather *Amy's* parents – are sending you to a different school, far away from here.'

'I suppose I could do that,' sighed Freddie. 'But I feel so dreadful about deceiving her! She's such a dear old lady.'

'Yes, but you're deceiving her for the best of reasons,' said June persuasively. 'Mrs Dale was awfully lonely, and now she's not. She's happy because she's got your visits to look forward to. That's good, isn't it?'

Freddie agreed, but without much conviction, and June smiled to herself. Poor Freddie had so much on her mind that she was in no mood for jokes and tricks. Everything was working out just as she had hoped!

The third formers had a lot to look forward to, for as well as June's trick, the following weekend was half-term.

'Are your parents coming, Bonnie?' asked Amy.

'Oh, yes,' answered Bonnie, who was putting the finishing touches to a skirt she had made. 'Mummy's simply dying to see the school – and me, of course.'

As Amy watched Bonnie expertly finish a hem, her needle flying in and out, she said admiringly, 'How clever you are with your needle, Bonnie. I do wish that you would make something for me.'

Bonnie smiled angelically at the girl and said sweetly, 'I will. If you will do something for me in return.'

Amy, who was used to people agreeing to whatever she asked immediately, and was unaccustomed to bargaining, looked a little taken aback and asked, 'What is it you want me to do?'

Bonnie folded the skirt she had been working on neatly, and laid it to one side, before saying, 'Well, as you're no doubt aware, I'm not very good at French. It doesn't much matter when Mam'zelle Dupont takes us, because I can easily get round her. But Mam'zelle Rougier – well, I haven't worked out how to make her like me yet.'

'Mam'zelle Rougier always dislikes the girls who Mam'zelle Dupont likes,' said Amy. 'Veronica told me so. You'll *never* get her to like you.'

'Oh, I shall,' said Bonnie, with quiet certainty. 'I can always make adults like me. It's just that it takes longer to get round some than others. And in the meantime, Mam'zelle Rougier is being simply beastly to me. She returned all that work I did in prep the other night – pages and pages of it – and expects me to redo it all and hand it in to her at the end of the week. I simply can't do it.'

'So, you want me to help you with your French, and you'll make me a dress, is that it?' said Amy.

Bonnie nodded. 'If you will do that for me, we can pop into town one lunchtime and choose a pattern and some material.'

As Amy found French easy, she agreed to this readily and both girls were happy. Someone who was not happy with this arrangement, however, was Veronica. It seemed that Amy and Bonnie were growing closer, while she, Veronica, was being pushed out. She would have to put her thinking cap on, and try and find a way of getting rid of Bonnie. And she had something else on her mind, too. With half-term almost upon them, Veronica needed to come up with a plan to keep her parents away so that she might spend the day with Amy and her people. Veronica frowned. How could a term that had started so promisingly have gone so wrong?

Vanishing cream

There was a great deal of giggling and excited chatter as the third formers took their places in class the next morning and eagerly awaited the arrival of Mam'zelle Dupont.

'My word, this is going to be super!' chuckled Pam.

'Isn't it just!' said Felicity, with a grin. 'June, have you got everything ready?'

In answer, June held up the empty vanishing-cream pot Amy had given her, and the key to the little storage room. She had sneaked into the handyman's room earlier, while he was out, and taken it from the nail on the wall. With luck, she would have it back there before he even noticed it was missing!

But luck was against June that morning. For the mistress who swept into the room was not plump little Mam'zelle Dupont, but Mam'zelle Rougier! The girls looked at one another in dismay, and murmurs of disappointment rippled round the room.

'What a shame!' Susan whispered to June. 'You won't be able to play the trick now.'

June glanced at the stern face of Mam'zelle Rougier. She hated the idea of all her careful planning being in vain. What was more, if she went ahead now, she would have the distinction of being the only girl in the school ever to have the nerve to play a trick on Mam'zelle Rougier, and that thought appealed to her enormously! She would probably be punished for it, but it would be worth it. She winked at Susan and whispered back, 'Just watch me!'

The word went round, murmured from girl to girl.

'The trick is still on! June's going to play it on Mam'zelle Rougier!'

'You have to admire her nerve.'

'She's sure to be punished, but June won't care. I don't think she's afraid of anything!'

'June is the most daring girl in the school – even more daring than her cousin Alicia was. And her tricks are simply splendid!'

June overheard the whispered remarks and revelled in them. No other girl could hold a candle to her when it came to playing tricks – not even Freddie.

Mam'zelle Rougier also heard the whispers – though fortunately she didn't catch what was being said – and her lips tightened into a thin line as she rapped sharply on the desk with a ruler, making everyone jump.

'*Taisez-vous!*' she commanded, in her rather harsh voice. 'Now, Mam'zelle Dupont has been awake all night with the toothache, and has gone to the dentist. So I shall be taking your French class this morning.'

Her sharp eyes swept round the classroom. She looked tired and irritable, which indeed she was, for her bedroom was next to Mam'zelle Dupont's and the other French mistress had kept her awake most of the night with her moans and groans. Mam'zelle Rougier put a hand across her mouth to hide a yawn, then said, 'Bonnie!'

'Yes, Mam'zelle?' said Bonnie politely.

'Bring to me the prep which I gave you back,' said Mam'zelle Rougier. 'And let us hope that you have managed to get *some* of it correct this time! The rest of you, turn to page 21 in your French grammar books and begin reading, *s'il vous plait*.'

Bonnie picked up her French book, into which she had carefully copied Amy's work, and stood up. She glanced round briefly at June, who winked, then went up to the mistress's desk and stood in front of it, so that Mam'zelle Rougier's view of the class was obscured.

Then June slipped from her seat and into the little storage room, which she had unlocked earlier.

At last Mam'zelle Rougier finished checking Bonnie's work, remarking grudgingly, 'A much better effort, Bonnie. Please return to your seat.'

The little girl skipped back to her place and Mam'zelle Rougier got to her feet, saying, 'Now, let us –'

Then she stopped, frowning, and said sharply, 'Where is June?'

'I'm here, Mam'zelle Rougier,' came June's disembodied voice.

'*Tiens!*' cried the French mistress. 'June, are you hiding under your desk? I demand that you come out at once!'

'I'm not *under* my desk, Mam'zelle,' said June from the storage room. 'I'm *at* my desk. Can't you see me?'

Nora, who was very good at acting, raised her hand and

said in a scared voice, 'Mam'zelle Rougier, June seems to have become invisible!'

The French mistress gave a snort of disbelief and snapped, 'What nonsense is this? June, I command you to show yourself.'

'But Mam'zelle, I'm here!' said June rather plaintively.

Most of the girls were struggling not to laugh by this time and, had the victim of the prank been Mam'zelle Dupont, they would have been in fits of giggles. But it was decidedly dangerous to laugh at the bad-tempered Mam'zelle Rougier, who was growing angrier by the second, so they did their best to control themselves.

The French mistress stalked to the back of the class, a frown on her face, and passed her hand over June's chair, before bending over and peering under the desk. This was too much for Susan, who gave a choke of laughter, which she hastily turned into a cough. Then Mam'zelle spotted the empty pot of vanishing cream that June had left on her desk, and picked it up.

'*Tiens!* What is this?' she asked.

Freddie, who, in spite of her worries, was thoroughly enjoying the trick, said, 'It's June's vanishing cream, Mam'zelle Rougier. Oh, I say! What if she's used too much and vanished for good!'

'Vanishing cream? Pah, what nonsense!' said the French mistress. All the same, she did look rather alarmed when she took the lid from the pot and saw that it was empty.

'She's used it all!' said Nora, sounding horrified. 'Mam'zelle Rougier, what are we to do?'

'Yes, what if she doesn't come back and stays invisible forever?' put in Pam.

'I will not have girls vanishing into thin air in my lesson!' cried Mam'zelle Rougier. Several of the listening girls found this so funny that they had to stuff handkerchiefs into their mouths to stifle their laughter.

'I shall go and inform Miss Grayling at once that June has disappeared,' said Mam'zelle Rougier, turning sharply and walking towards the door. As soon as her back was turned, June quietly sneaked from her hiding-place and back into her seat.

'Mam'zelle Rougier!' cried Felicity. 'She's back! June is visible again! There's no need for you to go to Miss Grayling.'

The French mistress looked round and gave a start as she saw the wicked June, sitting at her desk as large as life.

'June!' she cried. 'How dare you leave the classroom in the middle of a lesson.'

'But Mam'zelle, I didn't leave,' protested June. 'I was here all the time.'

'That's true, Mam'zelle,' said Julie. 'We all heard her voice.'

'Yes, but I do not wish to hear *your* voice, *ma chère* Julie!' said Mam'zelle Rougier, who was working herself up into a fine rage. 'June, I am not so easy to fool as Mam'zelle Dupont! I know that a trick has been played, and when I find out how you have made yourself vanish and then reappear I shall punish you!'

With that, Mam'zelle Rougier stalked back to the

blackboard, her heels click-clacking on the floor. And June, as fast as lightning, darted from her seat and back into the storage room. Mam'zelle Rougier turned to face the class, and gave a shriek, pressing her hands to her cheeks. '*Mon Dieu!* The troublesome girl has vanished again!'

'Sorry, Mam'zelle.' Once more June's voice could be heard from thin air. 'But I really can't help it.'

Well, the girls were quite helpless with laughter by this time, and past caring about any punishment that Mam'zelle Rougier might dish out. This was such an excellent trick that it would be well worth it! Tears rolled down Felicity's cheeks, while Susan was doubled up. Even Veronica was laughing uproariously!

'Silence!' shouted Mam'zelle Rougier, stamping her foot so hard that a strand of hair came down from the bun she wore at the back of her head. 'I will not tolerate this behaviour, *méchantes filles!* You will all write me fifty lines tonight!'

This sobered the third formers a little and their laughter died away. But just then the door of the classroom opened, and Mam'zelle Dupont appeared in the doorway. The relief of having her aching tooth removed had put the little French mistress in an excellent mood, and she beamed round at the girls.

'*Bonjour, mes petites! Bonjour*, Mam'zelle Rougier! I must thank you for taking my class while I was away, for I know that you, too, had a restless night and must be tired. Ah, my tooth, how it ached! But now it is all gone.'

'That is not all that is gone, Mam'zelle Dupont!' said

Mam'zelle Rougier dramatically. 'You will step outside with me, please, for I have a strange tale to tell.'

As soon as the two French mistresses had left the room, June emerged from the little room once more, this time locking the door behind her and slipping the key into her pocket.

'My word, June, that was a super trick!' exclaimed Nora, as June sat down behind her desk. 'But Mam'zelle Rougier is simply furious!'

'Yes, I'm afraid that you're going to get into awful trouble, June,' said Felicity.

'No, I'm not,' said June, grinning wickedly. 'An idea came to me when I heard Mam'zelle Dupont say that Mam'zelle Rougier had suffered a restless night. I think I can get us all off doing lines as well. Freddie, take that empty pot and throw it out of the window into the bushes. Now, listen, everyone – this is what we're going to do . . .'

Moments later, the two French mistresses returned, and Mam'zelle Rougier was most astonished to see June, looking the picture of goodness, with her head bent over her book.

'Ah! See, Mam'zelle Dupont!' she cried, clutching at the other French mistress's arm with one hand, and pointing at June with the other.

'Yes, I see June, sitting at her desk and working hard at her French,' said Mam'zelle Dupont, eyeing Mam'zelle Rougier with concern. The tale that she had related had been quite astonishing, and Mam'zelle Dupont was rather worried about her countrywoman's state of mind. Girls did not vanish and re-appear at random – it was quite impossible!

The other third formers appeared to be concentrating hard on their work too, the dear, good girls, and surely this would not be so if something was amiss with one of their friends.

'June, you have come back!' cried Mam'zelle Rougier.

'Come back?' repeated June, with a puzzled frown. 'But, Mam'zelle, I haven't been away.'

'Ah, but yes, you vanished!' said Mam'zelle Rougier. 'You put the vanishing cream on and you disappeared. The other girls, they saw you turn invisible – is it not so, girls?'

The third formers looked at one another in bewilderment and Felicity said, 'Mam'zelle Rougier, June has been here all the time.'

'Vanishing cream?' said Julie with a puzzled frown. 'What vanishing cream, Mam'zelle?'

'Ah, you are bad girls, all of you!' cried Mam'zelle Rougier, marching over to June's desk. 'You are all trying to trick me. June, where is the vanishing cream? Open your desk at once.'

June obeyed, but there was nothing to be seen in the desk but books, pens and pencils.

'You have hidden it in your satchel, then!' said Mam'zelle Rougier, quite beside herself. 'I demand to search it!'

So June handed over her satchel but, of course, the pot of vanishing cream was not in there either. Poor Mam'zelle Rougier did not know what to think! Were the girls playing an elaborate joke on her, or was she going quite mad?

At last June said kindly, 'I think I know what has happened. You must have been dreaming, Mam'zelle.'

'June, please do not speak rubbish to me!' said the French mistress scornfully. 'How is it possible for me to dream when I am wide awake?'

Once more the girls looked at one another and Felicity said solemnly, 'You fell asleep at your desk, Mam'zelle Rougier. It was right after Bonnie brought her book to you.'

'Never have I fallen asleep in a class!' said Mam'zelle Rougier, looking mortified.

'But you did, Mam'zelle,' said Susan. 'We wouldn't have said anything about it if you hadn't started talking about June vanishing.'

'Ah, this is my fault!' cried Mam'zelle Dupont. 'For it was I who kept you awake last night, Mam'zelle Rougier. It is no wonder that you fall asleep at your desk! Now, you must go back to bed for the rest of the morning, and catch up on your sleep. I shall take your next class and all will be well.'

So Mam'zelle Rougier, now convinced that the whole episode had been a strange dream, went quietly from the room.

'And the best of it is that she thinks the lines she gave us were part of the dream too!' laughed Nora. 'Well done, June.'

'Yes, that was a splendid trick,' said Freddie, taking June's arm. 'It quite took me out of myself for a while. And no one else could have carried it off like you, June. I take my hat off to you!'

Somehow, word spread around the school that June had successfully tricked Mam'zelle Rougier. Even the sixth form got to hear about it, and Amanda Chartelow came up to June with a broad grin on her face. 'Don't forget you've got lacrosse practice this afternoon,' she said. 'We don't want you doing one of your vanishing acts!'

Bonnie also took advantage of June's trick to get on the right side of Mam'zelle Rougier. She picked a huge bunch of late-blooming flowers from the garden and took them to the French mistress later that day.

'Oh, Mam'zelle Rougier, I've been so worried about you!' she said in her soft voice. 'I often used to have trouble sleeping when I was ill, and I know how tired it makes you the next day.'

Surprised and rather touched, Mam'zelle Rougier took the flowers from Bonnie, saying, 'Thank you, *ma chère*. This is indeed most kind of you.'

Bonnie smiled her most charming smile at the mistress and went on her way. And from that day on, Mam'zelle Rougier remembered the girl's thoughtfulness and was much kinder to her in class.

'So there's only Miss Peters who you haven't managed to charm,' said Nora in the common-room one evening. 'And she's a really tough nut to crack. You'll never succeed with her, Bonnie.'

'I bet you a stick of toffee I will,' said Bonnie at once.

'You're on!' said Nora. 'If you haven't managed to wrap Miss Peters round your little finger by the end of term that's a stick of toffee you owe me!'

Half-term

Half-term arrived at last, and there was great excitement throughout the school. Even sleepyheads like Nora and Amy leaped out of bed early, looking forward to the day with eager anticipation. Felicity was simply dying to see her mother and father, while Bonnie couldn't wait to be spoiled by her doting parents once more. And Amy was looking forward to showing off her good-looking father and beautiful mother to the others. Only Veronica looked forward to the day with mixed feelings, for try as she might, she had been quite unable to think of a way to put her parents off coming for half-term. It wasn't that she didn't love her mother and father, for she did. But she didn't feel that they were quite good enough for her – and they certainly weren't good enough to meet Amy's people!

As it turned out, fate took a hand and, just as the first parents were arriving, Veronica was called to Miss Grayling's office.

'Veronica, I'm afraid I have some disappointing news for you,' said the Head, after she had greeted the girl. 'Your father telephoned me earlier, and I'm afraid that he and your mother won't be able to come today. You see, your mother has flu and, although they were hoping that she would feel well enough to travel today, she is still quite ill.'

'I see,' said Veronica, beginning to feel a little guilty. She had wanted something to happen to stop her parents coming, but she certainly hadn't wished for her mother to be ill! 'Mother will be all right, won't she?' she asked the Head a little anxiously.

'Of course, my dear,' said Miss Grayling kindly. 'She just needs plenty of rest at the moment, and I daresay she will be as right as rain in a few days. Now off you go and join the others – and try to enjoy half-term as best you can.'

Reassured that her mother wasn't seriously ill, Veronica made up her mind to do just that! Amy was sure to invite her to go along with her people, and Veronica would be at pains to impress them. Perhaps they might even invite her to stay with them during the holidays!

Bonnie was in for a disappointment too, for she received a message to say that her parents' car had broken down, and they had to wait for it to be fixed, so they wouldn't arrive at Malory Towers until tomorrow.

'Well, at least you'll have *one* day with them,' said Felicity, seeing the girl's unhappy face. 'That's better than nothing. Cheer up, Bonnie!'

'I do feel sorry for her,' Felicity confided to Susan, as the girl walked away. 'But at the same time, I hope Mother doesn't ask her to join us. Does that sound awfully selfish?'

'Of course not,' said Susan loyally. 'It's quite understandable that you want to have your parents to yourself at half-term. I know that I wouldn't want to share mine with Bonnie!'

'I say!' called out Pam, who was stationed at the dormitory window. 'There are some more cars coming up the drive. My word, just look at that Rolls Royce!'

'Why, that must belong to my people!' cried Amy, almost knocking Julie over in her eagerness to get to the window. 'Yes, it's them! I must go down and greet them.'

'Felicity, I think your parents are here too,' said Pam. 'And mine are right behind them – whoopee! Come on, let's go down.'

Soon the grounds were thronged with laughing, chattering girls and their families. As she chatted happily with her parents, Felicity saw Julie, with her mother and older brother, both of them red-haired and freckled, like Julie herself. Then she spotted Pam, walking arm-in-arm with her parents, and June, sharing a joke with one of her brothers. And over there, talking to Mam'zelle Rougier, was Amy, with her mother. Felicity couldn't help glancing at Mrs Ryder-Cochrane curiously. She was every bit as lovely as she appeared in her photograph, but the cat-like green eyes gave her rather a sly look, and Felicity decided that she didn't like her very much. Susan's big, jovial father was standing nearby, and Felicity saw, with a shock, that the man he was having a conversation with was Mr Ryder-Cochrane. And Amy's father didn't fit with the image that Felicity had built up in her mind at all! He was a most distinguished man, and at the moment he looked very relaxed and carefree, and was laughing heartily at something that Susan's father had said. Nothing could have been further from the cold, snobbish man that

111

Felicity had been imagining. Amy's father must be a very good actor indeed! Just then Mr Ryder-Cochrane caught her looking at him and grinned. But Felicity, thinking suddenly of Mrs Dale, and of how lonely and unhappy she was because of this man, could only manage a tight, polite little smile in return, before she turned away.

Freddie, too, had noticed Amy's parents, but she could barely bring herself to look at them, for she felt intensely angry with the couple. If it wasn't for Mr Ryder-Cochrane's stupid, stuck-up attitude and Mrs Ryder-Cochrane's weakness in not standing up to her husband, she wouldn't be in the uncomfortable situation she was in now!

At Mrs Dale's request, Freddie had visited her yesterday afternoon, and had left feeling guiltier than ever. The visit had been highly enjoyable to start with, and Freddie and Mrs Dale had chatted about all kinds of things. But then the old lady had begun recounting bits of family history, and had brought out some photographs of Amy's mother as a child, and Freddie had felt most uncomfortable – almost as if she was stealing a bit of Amy's life. Now, she was delighted to be with her own loving, sensible parents, and hugged them extra hard. She was determined not to let her guilt cast a shadow over the day, and to enjoy herself, but it was very difficult. How she wished that she could confide in her mother and father about Mrs Dale, but that was impossible of course. They would be so terribly disappointed in her!

As the day went on, Bonnie and Veronica, being the only two in the third form whose parents hadn't come, found themselves thrown together, which pleased neither of them! Big-hearted Mam'zelle Dupont, seeing them hovering on the edge of the crowd, bore down on them and said sympathetically, 'Ah, *les pauvres petites*! Do not be sad while all the others are out with their so-dear parents. We will have a splendid lunch in the school dining-room, and the two of you will sit with me, *n'est-ce pas*?'

Veronica nodded politely and Bonnie smiled her sweet smile, but both of them were hoping to be invited out to lunch. Bonnie had already dropped broad hints to Felicity and her parents, but Mr and Mrs Rivers, obedient to the silent message in Felicity's eyes, had steadfastly ignored them. So both girls' hopes now centred on Amy, who was coming towards them with her parents.

Amy introduced her parents to the two girls and, while Mrs Ryder-Cochrane greeted Bonnie, her husband turned to Veronica and attempted to make polite conversation. But alas for Veronica, Amy's father seemed so very grand that she became quite tongue-tied, unable to mutter anything but 'yes' or 'no' in answer to his questions. Bonnie, however, was determined to make a hit with the couple, and she looked at Amy's mother with undisguised admiration, complimenting her on her expensive dress and perfectly groomed hair. Mrs Ryder-Cochrane, who had been looking a little bored, thawed visibly and decided that Bonnie was rather a dear little thing.

'Bonnie is the girl I wrote to you about, Mummy,' said Amy. 'The one who makes such beautiful clothes.'

Veronica listened to this rather glumly. It seemed that

she hadn't been mentioned in Amy's letters home at all. And she didn't like the way that Mrs Ryder-Cochrane seemed to have taken to Bonnie. She tapped the smaller girl on the shoulder and said, 'It's almost lunchtime, Bonnie. We'd better go and get ready.'

'Of course,' said Bonnie, managing to make her smile both brave and pathetic. 'Oh, *how* I wish that *my* mother and father were here to take me out to a restaurant. Still, I'm quite sure that the school lunch will be delicious. Come along, Veronica.'

As the two girls walked off towards the school, Mrs Ryder-Cochrane said in a low voice to Amy, 'Why don't you ask little Bonnie to come out with us, darling? She seems such a sweet girl.'

'Oh, Mummy, can I?' said Amy, her eyes lighting up. She always enjoyed basking in her beautiful mother's reflected glory, and had been thrilled by how impressed with her Bonnie had seemed. 'I'll go and tell her now.'

'What about the other girl?' said Mr Ryder-Cochrane. 'It seems a bit mean to leave her behind. Amy, you had better invite her too.'

But Amy was already speeding off after Bonnie, and didn't hear what her father had said.

'Bonnie!' she cried, catching up with the two girls. 'Mummy says that you're to come out to lunch with us. You'd better let Miss Peters know, or she might think you've gone missing, but do hurry up.'

Then she dashed back to her parents, while Bonnie went off in search of Miss Peters. Veronica was left alone, looking very forlorn, and Felicity, who was in earshot, felt sorry for her. 'Really,' she thought indignantly. 'Amy might have asked Veronica along too!'

Something about the slump of the girl's shoulders as she turned away went straight to Felicity's heart and she made an impulsive decision. Without giving herself time to think about whether she would regret it later, Felicity ran over to Veronica and grabbed her arm, saying, 'Veronica, go and get ready – you're coming out with me and my people!'

For a moment Veronica thought that she had misheard Felicity, and she could only stand staring at her blankly. Felicity gave her a little shake and said, 'You do want to come, don't you? It's nothing grand, just a picnic lunch and a walk along the beach, but it's better than being here on your own.'

Veronica found her voice at last, stammering out her thanks, but Felicity cut her short, saying, 'Never mind that! Go and fetch your coat, while I run and let Miss Peters know what's happening. I'll meet you back here in five minutes!'

If Mr and Mrs Rivers were a little surprised to find that Felicity had invited a strange girl to share their picnic, they were far too well-mannered to betray it, and did their utmost to make Veronica feel welcome.

As they were getting into the car, Amy, her parents and Bonnie drove past, the two girls looking most surprised to see Felicity and Veronica together.

'How odd!' remarked Amy. 'I always thought that Veronica couldn't bear Felicity.'

'And I thought that Felicity couldn't bear Veronica,' said Bonnie, who felt quite jealous at seeing the two girls together. Why on earth had Felicity asked Veronica out instead of her, Bonnie? The girl brooded on it during the drive to the restaurant. Perhaps she had been spending too much time with Amy and neglecting Felicity. Although it had been Felicity's idea for her to make friends with Amy in the first place, so she ought to understand. But Bonnie had, in her own way, become quite fond of Amy as their friendship grew, and she certainly enjoyed her company. Maybe Felicity had sensed this, and had gone off with Veronica to get back at Bonnie. Yes, that was the only sensible explanation, for Felicity couldn't possibly *like* Veronica! Bonnie made up her mind that she would devote more time to Felicity when they got back to school, and show her that their friendship was still important to her.

Felicity, meanwhile, mercifully unaware of Bonnie's intentions, was having a simply marvellous time. And so, for a wonder, was Veronica. The girl had been a little stiff and shy with Mr and Mrs Rivers at first, but they were such a charming couple that this very soon wore off. She took a particular liking to Mrs Rivers, whose warm, friendly manner put her very much in mind of her own mother. As she walked along the beach beside Mrs Rivers, watching Felicity and Mr Rivers looking for shells a little way in front, a pang of conscience smote Veronica. How *could* she have been so stupid and wicked as to wish that her parents wouldn't be able to come today? Well, she had got her wish and now she had an overwhelming desire to see her mother, and speak to her. Her father too. She gave a sigh and Mrs Rivers asked kindly, 'Is anything wrong, dear?'

'I was just thinking about my parents,' said Veronica with a rather wobbly smile. 'And hoping that my mother isn't feeling too poorly.'

'Poor child,' said Felicity's mother, taking her hand. Then an idea occurred to her. 'Why don't you ask Miss Grayling if you can use her telephone to call them tonight? I'm sure that she wouldn't mind, under the circumstances. And you'll sleep better tonight after you've had a little chat with your parents, knowing that your mother is being looked after.'

Veronica brightened at once and said, 'Oh, that would be simply marvellous. Do you really think the Head would let me?'

'Well, if you like, Veronica, I will come along to Miss Grayling's office with you when we get back to Malory Towers,' offered Mrs Rivers. 'I am quite sure that she won't refuse.'

'Thank you, Mrs Rivers,' said Veronica simply. 'You have been so kind to me today.'

Veronica went up to Felicity in the dormitory that evening and thanked her too.

'It was jolly decent of you to invite me,' she said. 'I had a wonderful time – and I think you're very lucky to have such super parents.'

'I think I am too,' said Felicity with a smile, marvelling at the change in Veronica. Mrs Rivers had stuck to her word and asked Miss Grayling if the girl might telephone

117

her parents. The Head had agreed at once, of course, and Veronica had felt much easier in her mind after talking to her father, and learning that her mother was feeling a little better. She had come into the common-room afterwards with a beaming smile on her face, and the third formers had looked at her in surprise.

'I've seen a different side to Veronica today,' Felicity had said to Susan. 'She seemed much – oh, I don't know – much softer and more humble somehow.'

June, sitting nearby, had given a scornful snort and said, 'Don't let her fool you, Felicity. You're too soft-hearted for your own good!'

'So you keep telling me!' said Felicity, nettled. 'But I think that only a *hard*-hearted person could have failed to feel sorry for Veronica today. It must have been dreadful for her being alone, when most of us had our people here.'

'She's putting on an act to gain sympathy,' scoffed June. 'Of course, what she *really* wanted was *Amy*'s sympathy – and lunch in a fancy restaurant. But that didn't work, so she had to fall back on you, Felicity. Veronica will be back to her old self again before long, you mark my words!'

'Perhaps the two of you should agree to disagree,' said the sensible, steady Susan, looking from Felicity's troubled little face to June's mocking one. 'Come on now – it's been a super day. Let's not spoil it with a silly argument.'

'Dear Susan!' said June with a laugh. 'Always pouring oil on troubled waters. No, don't glare at me like that, Felicity, for I have no intention of arguing with you. As Susan has so sensibly suggested, we'll agree to disagree.'

And the matter was left there, though Felicity still felt a little cross with June. The trouble was, she thought, June was always so sure of herself that she made those less confident – like Felicity – doubt their own opinions! So when Veronica came over in the dormitory and thanked her, Felicity felt heartened.

But the next day, Sunday, saw Veronica at Amy's side again. Bonnie's parents arrived to take her out, so Amy graciously invited Veronica to spend the day with her and her parents.

Felicity, unaware of this invitation, sought out Veronica and said generously, 'You know, Veronica, you're most welcome to come with me and my people again today.'

'That's awfully kind of you, Felicity,' said Veronica, blushing and looking a little awkward. 'But, you see, Amy has already invited me to spend the day with her and I've accepted.'

'Oh, well, that's up to you, of course,' said Felicity, with a careless shrug. Inwardly, though, she wondered how Veronica could have such little pride that she tagged along with Amy after the girl had so callously abandoned her yesterday.

Still, it was none of her business really, and it would be nice to have her parents all to herself. All the same, she hoped that June wasn't going to be proved right about Veronica. She was far too cocksure as it was!

Trouble in the third form

'Everything seems so flat after half-term,' complained Nora, as the third formers stood in the courtyard one break-time. 'I need cheering up! June, can't you play another trick?'

'No, you've had two this term already,' answered June. 'I don't want to spoil you. Besides, if we play too many tricks they just end up becoming commonplace and people don't appreciate them as they should.'

'Spoilsport!' said Nora, pulling a face. 'How about you then, Freddie? Can't you come up with something to give us all a laugh?'

But Freddie, who seemed to be in a world of her own, hadn't been listening to the conversation and didn't even realise that Nora was addressing her until June gave her a nudge.

'Sorry, Nora,' said Freddie, sounding distracted. 'What did you say?'

Nora repeated her request, but Freddie shook her head and said ruefully, 'I don't seem to be able to come up with any jokes or tricks at the moment, I'm afraid.'

Felicity frowned at this. Freddie's sense of fun certainly seemed to have deserted her lately. She said as much to

Susan, when the two of them were alone in the common-room later.

'She doesn't seem like her old, jolly self,' Susan agreed. 'Perhaps she's finding it a bit of a strain to keep up with June, who can do brilliantly at lessons *and* play the fool. But Freddie isn't quite as clever as June, and she needs to concentrate more in class to get good results.'

'Yes, you're probably right,' said Felicity, her brow clearing. 'Darrell used to say that Alicia was just the same. Let's hope that's all it is, anyway.'

'I saw you talking to Bonnie earlier,' said Susan, changing the subject. 'She seems to be hanging round you more and more since half-term.'

'Yes, I *had* noticed,' said Felicity wearily. 'She keeps trying to persuade me to make up a three with her and Amy, and no matter how often I refuse, she always comes back. I must say, for someone so dainty and fragile-looking, she's awfully thick-skinned!'

'Well, thank goodness we managed to get her to spend some time with Amy,' said Susan. 'Otherwise I should *never* have you to myself.'

'Yes, that little scheme worked a treat,' said Felicity. 'Though I don't suppose Bonnie would be too pleased if she knew that I had only suggested she try to split Amy and Veronica up because we didn't want her tagging along with us all the time! And Veronica would be simply furious too.'

'Well, thank goodness neither of them *will* find out,' said Susan complacently.

But she was quite wrong. For at that very moment, Veronica was standing on the other side of the common-room door! As usual, she hadn't *meant* to listen, and had only been on her way to the common-room to collect something. But on hearing voices, the urge to listen in had been too much. And now her feelings were very mixed. On the one hand, the knowledge that Bonnie had only befriended Amy as a favour to Felicity would be very useful indeed. But she also felt hurt and angry that Felicity had set Bonnie to work to break up her own friendship with Amy. Since half-term her feelings towards Felicity had softened a great deal, but now the old feelings of bitterness and resentment came flooding back. Just who did Felicity Rivers think she was? Well, she was in for a shock – and so was silly little Bonnie!

Bonnie grew quite exasperated with Veronica over the next couple of days. The girl kept giving her strange looks, and odd, triumphant little smiles that Bonnie was quite at a loss to understand. Veronica, typically, was enjoying savouring her new-found knowledge and keeping it to herself, until the moment was right to break the news to Amy. And the moment came after art lesson one afternoon.

Miss Linnie, the art mistress, was very good-natured and easy-going, and the girls were allowed to sit where they pleased in her class. Amy took a seat by the window, and both Veronica and Bonnie moved towards the empty seat beside her. Bonnie reached it first and sat down, much to Veronica's annoyance.

'I always sit next to Amy!' she protested.

'Well, it will be a pleasant change for her to have me beside her instead,' said Bonnie softly, looking up at Veronica with the innocent stare that always infuriated her. 'Off you go, Veronica.'

But Veronica wasn't giving up without a fight, and she said through gritted teeth, 'I'm not going anywhere, you little beast. Move at once!'

Amy, who loved to have people fighting over her favours, took no part in the quarrel, but stared rather smugly out of the window. It was left to Miss Linnie to intervene, saying calmly but firmly, 'That will do, girls! Veronica, there is a seat over there next to Julie. Please go and sit there.'

Veronica did not dare disobey the mistress, and reluctantly moved away to sit next to Julie, leaving Bonnie to enjoy her victory.

Miss Linnie's classes were always very free and easy, and the girls chattered away to one another as they worked. Veronica scowled as she watched Amy and Bonnie, their heads together as they talked and laughed. Well, Bonnie would be laughing on the other side of her face very soon!

After the art lesson finished, Veronica caught up with Amy and Bonnie outside.

'I do so love Miss Linnie's classes, don't you?' said Bonnie sweetly. 'Amy and I just talked and talked throughout the whole lesson.'

'Really?' said Veronica, a smile on her face and a

dangerous glint in her eyes. 'And did you talk about how you have only been sucking up to Amy because Felicity Rivers put you up to it?'

Bonnie turned pale, while Amy gasped and said, 'Bonnie, is this true?'

'It – it's true that Felicity asked me to try and make friends with you,' stammered Bonnie. Then she threw a spiteful look at Veronica and went on, 'She wanted me to try and get you away from dear Veronica's unpleasant influence. But I did genuinely like you from the first, Amy, and now that I know you better I like you even more. Please say that we can still be friends!'

Amy was quivering with indignation. She was used to people vying for her friendship, and to hear that Bonnie had only palled up with her because Felicity had put her up to it, was very hard for her to bear.

'I think I'll stick with Veronica,' she said, her tone icy. 'At least I know that *she* is a true friend. Come along, Veronica.'

'Just a moment,' said Veronica. 'Bonnie, there's something I need to tell you. You see, the main reason that Felicity asked you to befriend Amy was that she and Susan were sick to death of you following them round all the time and making a nuisance of yourself. Quite honestly, I can't say that I blame them.'

Stricken and longing to get back at Veronica, Bonnie snapped, 'And just how did you find all this out, Veronica? Through spying on people and listening at doors, I expect.' Veronica's guilty look told Bonnie at once that she had hit the nail on the head, and she said scornfully, 'I thought as much. You're despicable, Veronica!'

'Well I, for one, am extremely glad that Veronica *did* find all this out,' said Amy haughtily. 'Otherwise I should never have found out what a deceitful little creature you are, Bonnie.'

And with that, she took Veronica's arm and the two girls walked away, leaving Bonnie alone with her thoughts. Alas, they were not happy ones. She had lost Amy's friendship, and now it seemed that Felicity didn't want her either. Poor Bonnie gave a little sob. Was that what Felicity really thought of her – that she was nothing but a nuisance? And did she honestly prefer the company of that dull, boring Susan? Well, there was only one way to find out for sure – and that was to tackle Felicity.

The third-form common-room was very crowded and noisy that evening. Nora had put a gramophone record on, and she and Pam were doing an idiotic dance to the music, keeping the others in fits of laughter. As the music stopped, Bonnie raised her voice and said, 'Felicity! I need to speak to you. Is it true that you only encouraged me to be Amy's friend because you wanted me to leave you alone?'

Felicity bit her lip, seeing the hurt and anger in the other girl's eyes. But it was no use beating around the bush. The time had come to be straight with Bonnie.

'Yes,' she said. 'It's true. I'm sorry if you're upset, Bonnie, but I did try to let you down gently. You just wouldn't take the hint.'

The rest of the third form had gone quiet now, all of them listening intently as Felicity went on, 'Susan is my best friend, and you knew that from the start. And she always will be. No one can take her place with me.' Then, seeing that Bonnie looked as if she was about to burst into tears, she added more gently, 'You and I have very little in common, Bonnie, whereas you and Amy are interested in the same things. It's right that the two of you should be friends.'

'Excuse me, Felicity!' said Amy angrily, jumping to her feet. 'I prefer to choose my own friends, if you don't mind. And I most certainly do *not* want to be friends with a girl who has only been nice to me as a favour to you!'

And Amy flounced out of the room, slamming the door behind her.

Susan, who had been listening to all of this with a frown, said, 'Felicity and I never meant you to find out about this, Bonnie, and I'm sorry that you and Amy have fallen out because of it.'

'How *did* you find out?' asked Felicity, who had been puzzling over this.

'Veronica told me,' answered Bonnie, with a malicious glare in the direction of the culprit. 'I'll leave you to work out for yourself how she came by her information.'

Felicity rounded on Veronica at once, crying, 'So, you've been snooping again, Veronica! I did think, after I was nice to you at half-term, that you might have turned over a new leaf, but you're just as bad as ever.'

Several of the girls looked at Veronica in disgust and her

cheeks burned – until she remembered something else that she had overheard.

'It's just as well I did,' she retorted. 'For I found out that you egged Bonnie on to try and spoil my friendship with Amy. So don't dare act all high and mighty with me, Felicity Rivers!'

Then Veronica, too, stormed out of the room and June, who had been watching the dramatic scene avidly, laughed. 'Well done, Felicity!' she called out. 'That's two people you've managed to drive out of the room this evening.'

'Oh, shut up, June!' snapped Felicity, who was in no mood for June's malicious sense of humour tonight.

June said no more, but grinned as she lounged back in her chair, waiting for the entertainment to continue. Freddie looked hard at her friend, saw how she was thoroughly enjoying all the drama, and suddenly realised – with a little shock – that June thrived on trouble. And if life was going along too peacefully and smoothly, she would stir things up herself. For the first time a doubt crept into Freddie's mind. *Had* June been acting kindly and thinking of Mrs Dale's happiness when she suggested that she, Freddie, pose as Amy? Or had she used Freddie as a cat's-paw to play an outrageous prank that she had known would end in trouble? But there was no time to think about that now, for Bonnie had turned on Felicity again, her voice trembling as she cried, 'I hope you're satisfied, Felicity Rivers! *You* don't want to be my friend, and now – thanks to you – Amy doesn't either. I've got nobody! Nobody at all!'

Then she burst into noisy sobs and fled from the room, causing June to crow, 'A hat-trick! Nice work, Felicity!'

Seeing that the normally even-tempered Felicity looked ready to explode, Pam gave June a little shove and muttered, 'For heaven's sake, be quiet, June! Things are quite tense enough in here tonight as it is, without you stirring things up.'

'I shan't say another word, Pam,' said June, her eyes dancing mischievously. 'It looks as if our dear head-girl has quite enough on her plate at the moment, without me adding to her woes.'

Yes, and didn't June just relish the fact, thought Freddie, watching her through lowered eyelashes. If only she could make the laughing, carefree girl feel the weight of her conscience, just as she, Freddie, felt hers lying heavy on her shoulders. But did June even *have* a conscience? Freddie didn't know, but she intended to find out. And if it turned out that June *did* have one, Freddie was going to stir it into life!

Felicity felt very down in the dumps the following afternoon, as she and Susan got changed ready for lacrosse practice.

'I must be the only head-girl at Malory Towers ever to have been sent to Coventry by her own form,' she complained.

'What nonsense!' said Susan, laughing at her friend's gloomy expression. 'You haven't been sent to Coventry!'

'Well, Amy is barely speaking to me, while Bonnie and Veronica won't have anything to do with me at all,' Felicity sighed. 'And although I don't care for any of them very much, I can't altogether blame them. I really don't feel as if I've handled this very well.'

'Don't feel as if you've handled what very well?' asked Pam, coming into the changing-room in time to hear this.

Felicity told her, and finished by saying miserably, 'I don't think that I've been a great success as head-girl. Susan, you would have been a much better choice. Or you, Pam. You were absolutely fine last year.'

'Yes, but I was lucky,' said Pam, wrinkling her brow thoughtfully. 'Everything went really smoothly last year, and I didn't have people like Veronica, or Bonnie, or Amy to deal with. So you see, Felicity, I wasn't really tested.'

'Well, I've been tested all right,' groaned Felicity. 'And I've been found wanting.'

'There's still time to put things right,' said Pam bracingly. 'The term isn't over yet.'

'What Pam says is quite true,' said Susan. 'Everything will be sorted out in the end, Felicity, you'll see. Now come on, let's go and blow some of those cobwebs away on the lacrosse field. You know, Felicity, Amanda was telling me that you stand a jolly good chance of getting into the second team this year.'

'Did she really?' said Felicity, cheering up at once. 'Susan, you must practise hard too and let's see if we can both get on the team. Wouldn't that be simply marvellous?'

June had also been looking forward to lacrosse practice, but Freddie had other ideas.

'I told you, Mrs Dale has invited me to tea and she said

that I might bring a friend,' said Freddie. 'And the friend I'm bringing is you.'

'But Amanda's expecting me to turn up for lacrosse,' grumbled June, who didn't want to have tea with Mrs Dale at all. She had purposely distanced herself from the old lady and the situation she had created. But Freddie, seeing June through new eyes, was now aware of this and was determined that June wasn't going to keep her distance any longer.

'Amanda will understand,' she said firmly. 'It's Saturday, and the practice is optional, so you don't *have* to go. Besides, there's another one tomorrow afternoon if you're really that keen.'

June continued to protest, but for once Freddie was determined to have her way, and eventually the two set off together to Mrs Dale's. And, by the time they left, June's conscience was very much alive.

The girl started to feel a little guilty when Mrs Dale welcomed her warmly, as 'Amy's' friend, before sitting the two girls down to a simply sumptuous tea.

'Heavens, you must have been baking all morning!' exclaimed Freddie, her eyes staring at the table laden with homemade scones, cakes and apple pie.

'Well, it's nice having someone to cook for,' beamed the old lady. 'Now, tuck in, both of you.'

But, delicious as the food was, June found that her appetite had deserted her, and the food seemed to stick in her throat. This tea must have cost quite a lot of money, and it was obvious that Mrs Dale wasn't very well off. With a sinking heart, June remembered telling Freddie blithely what a sweet old lady Mrs Dale was. But June hadn't realised at the time *how* sweet and how kind she was. And what had seemed like a prank now began to feel like a very cruel deception. June also felt unnerved by the obvious, and very genuine, affection between Freddie and Mrs Dale, something that she hadn't bargained for. But worse was to come. As the girls were thinking about setting off back to Malory Towers, Mrs Dale suddenly exclaimed, 'Why, Amy, it's your birthday a week tomorrow, isn't it?'

Was it? thought Freddie, startled. Then she remembered hearing Amy mention something to Veronica about having a birthday coming up soon, and she nodded.

'Well, you must come over and I'll give you your present,' said Mrs Dale happily, as the two girls exchanged horrified glances.

'There's no need to give me a present, Gran,' said Freddie in a strangled tone. 'Please don't spend your money on me.'

'Well, what's the world coming to if I can't give my only granddaughter a present on her birthday!' tutted Mrs Dale. 'I've never heard the like!'

So the end of it was that Freddie had to promise to visit Mrs Dale on Amy's birthday, but she was deeply unhappy about it. And so was June. She was oddly silent on the walk back to Malory Towers, but inwardly she felt sick. She had meant to keep Freddie occupied, and had foreseen that the girl would begin to feel guilty about deceiving the old lady. But she – who prided herself so much on her careful planning – hadn't foreseen that the two would become so fond of one another, and she could have kicked herself. Not for the world would she willingly have hurt Mrs Dale – or Freddie either, for that matter. And the dreadful thing was, June couldn't see any way out of it without causing both of them a lot of pain. Nor could she fool herself into thinking that it was Freddie's problem and not hers. She was responsible for this whole, terrible mess, and somehow she had to think of a way to make everything right.

A shock for Amy

June felt very sorry for Freddie now that she understood some of what she had been going through, and knew how sickening it was to have something preying on your mind. It was really horrible, for even when you were laughing and joking with friends, it was always there, at the back of your mind, casting a dark shadow. But although she was kinder to Freddie, June's worries made her very short-tempered indeed with everyone else.

She went to Amanda's Sunday lacrosse practice, hoping for a respite from her cares, but unfortunately it only made things worse. The girl marking her, Fay, from South Tower, was an agile and most determined little player, and hardly allowed June near the ball at all. Frustrated, June lost her temper and tackled poor Fay most aggressively, knocking her to the ground and bringing Amanda's wrath down on her head.

'June!' cried Amanda, storming on to the field. 'Off! No, don't argue with me! Go and get changed at once.'

Angrily, June stomped off to the changing-room, but by the time she had got back into her uniform, her anger had deserted her and she felt deeply ashamed of herself. Amanda glared at her when she appeared among the spectators, but she was mollified when, at the end of the practice, June went up to Fay and apologised. She also said sorry to Amanda, and the big girl accepted her apology, saying, 'Very well, but you must learn to control your temper, June, for I can't possibly include you in a team until you do!'

But the next morning June was in hot water again, after cheeking Miss Peters in the Geography class.

'How dare you speak to me like that!' snapped the mistress, her rosy cheeks turning even redder, as they always did when she was angry. 'And stand up when I address you.'

Red-faced, June got sullenly to her feet and mumbled, 'I'm sorry, Miss Peters.'

'I beg your pardon, June?' said Miss Peters coldly, and June was forced to repeat her apology more clearly. Really, all she seemed to do lately was apologise to people!

'Come and see me after class,' said the mistress. 'When I shall have decided on a suitable punishment for you.'

And knowing Miss Peters, she wouldn't get off lightly, thought June, sitting down again.

As head of the form, Felicity took the girl to task for her behaviour, and June bore it as patiently as she could. Heavens, it wouldn't do if she fell out with Felicity as well! She really must try and concentrate on the problem that was causing her irritation, and not let her temper get the better of her.

Alas for such good intentions! June got in a rage again that very evening – this time with Amy.

Amy had been holding forth to a rapt Veronica in the common-room about her forthcoming birthday, and the others were getting heartily sick of her.

'As it's on a Sunday, Mummy and Daddy have got the Head's permission to come and take me out,' said Amy. 'We're going to that very grand hotel overlooking the beach for lunch, and they're sure to bring me a super present.'

Veronica exclaimed in admiration, and Amy went on, 'My aunt always sends me the most enormous cake, as well, so we can all share that at teatime. Did I ever tell you about the Christmas party they threw for my friends at home last year? My word, it was magnificent! We had –'

But at this point June, who had been trying to concentrate on the extra work Miss Peters had set her as punishment, threw down her book and leaped to her feet. 'Yes, Amy, you *did* tell Veronica about the marvellous party Mummy and Daddy threw for you!' she cried. 'And about the very expensive present they bought you, and about every birthday you've ever had since you were five years old! And I, for one, am sick and tired of hearing about it. You're nothing but a spoilt brat, Amy!'

Amy shrank back as though she had been slapped, while the others looked on in shocked silence. Amy *had* been annoying, but there was no need for June to be quite so vicious!

Felicity called her sharply to order and, had Amy not retaliated, the matter might have rested there.

But Amy, recovering from her shock, found her voice

and, looking down her long nose at June, she said, 'I suppose you're just jealous, June, because your parents aren't as wealthy as mine, and can't afford to throw splendid parties for you, or give you expensive presents.'

At once June fired up again and, without thinking, retorted, 'I'd rather have my parents than yours any day, Amy! Do you think I would want a father who is ashamed of my mother's family? Or a mother who is too weak to stand up to him? No, thank you!'

As soon as the words were out June regretted them and wished that she could take them back. But it was too late. Felicity and Susan were staring at her in horror. Freddie had turned pale, her hands tightly gripping the arms of her chair. And Amy was looking completely bewildered, as were the rest of the girls.

Contrite now, June said hastily, 'I'm sorry, Amy. Please forget that I said that. Honestly, I get into such a rage sometimes that I don't know *what* I'm saying half of the time!'

'I can't forget it,' said Amy, a queer look on her face. 'And I think that you knew exactly what you were saying, June. What did you mean?'

It was unlike June to be lost for words, but she was now and she looked at Felicity for help. And Felicity decided that it was no use trying to hide the truth from Amy any longer. She was absolutely furious with June for blurting it out like that, but she would deal with her later! As concisely as possible, she told Amy how she, Susan and June had met her grandmother, and how they had promised not to tell Amy that she was living near the school because she didn't want to go against Mr Ryder-Cochrane's wishes.

Amy listened intently, an incredulous expression on her face, and when Felicity had finished, she laughed and shook her head. 'You're mistaken, Felicity,' she said. 'My grandmother moved to Australia shortly before my parents married. And as for my father disapproving of her – why, that's nonsense! He promised me that we would go and visit her one day. In fact, we've been on the verge of going several times, but Mummy has always been taken ill, so it hasn't happened yet. I don't know who this woman is, but she certainly isn't my grandmother!'

The third formers didn't know what to think now, and exchanged puzzled looks. Then Pam, who had been looking very thoughtful, said, 'Amy, do you have a photograph of your grandmother?'

'Yes,' said Amy. 'It's one that she sent to Mummy from Australia.'

'Go and fetch it then,' said Pam. 'And hurry up!'

Amy rushed from the room, and was back a few moments later, clutching a photograph, which she handed to Felicity.

'It's Mrs Dale!' said Felicity. 'Amy, I tell you this is definitely the woman that Susan, June and I met. Isn't that so, Susan?'

Susan, who was peering over Felicity's shoulder at the photograph, nodded solemnly, and Nora said, 'The plot thickens. I say, Amy, I don't suppose your grandmother has a twin sister?'

'Of course she hasn't!' said Amy, her thoughts in a whirl. 'It doesn't make any sense. If Grandmother has returned from Australia, why hasn't she been in touch with me, or with Mummy? I don't understand what's going on!'

'I think I do,' said June, who had been looking very pensive. 'But I don't think you will like what I have to say, Amy.'

'Well, that doesn't usually bother you!' said Amy harshly. 'Just spit it out, June.'

'Very well,' said June, looking rather grave. 'You see, Amy, it isn't your father who is ashamed of Mrs Dale – it's your mother!'

As Amy remained speechless, her mouth wide open, June went on, 'Mrs Dale isn't at all wealthy or grand. I think that your mother was afraid to let your father meet her, because she didn't want him to know that she came from a plain, ordinary family. So she pretended that her mother lived in Australia, and then fooled you and your father into thinking she was ill every time a trip to visit Mrs Dale was planned.'

'I don't believe it,' said poor Amy, her face ashen. 'How could Mummy do that? And how could she lie to Daddy and to me for all this time?'

Everyone felt very sorry for Amy, and Felicity put a hand on the girl's shoulder, saying kindly, 'All of this must have come as a dreadful shock to you, Amy. I think that you ought to sort things out with your parents when they come for your birthday.'

But Amy hardly seemed to hear what Felicity said, for there was one thought uppermost in her mind and she said firmly, 'I want to meet my grandmother.'

'Well, you can't go and meet her now!' said Susan, sounding alarmed. 'It's dark and it's almost bedtime.'

'Tomorrow, then,' said Amy determinedly. 'Felicity, you can come with me and show me where she lives.'

Suddenly, Freddie, who had remained silent and lost in thought throughout, stood up and said firmly, 'I'll come with you, Amy.'

Every head turned towards her in astonishment, and Felicity said, 'You, Freddie? But you don't know Mrs Dale!'

'I do,' said Freddie, looking extremely white and nervous. 'Amy, I know you've had a great shock tonight, but I'm afraid you haven't heard everything. You see, Mrs Dale thinks that I am you.'

'This gets stranger and stranger by the second!' said Julie, scratching her head. 'Freddie, how can Mrs Dale possibly think that you are Amy?'

Stammering, her voice cracking, Freddie explained.

'Well!' exclaimed Pam, as Freddie reached the end of her tale and hung her head. 'This is certainly a night for revelations! Does anyone else have anything extraordinary they would like to own up to?'

No one did, of course, and Freddie went over to Amy, taking both of the girl's hands in hers and saying earnestly, 'Please let me come with you tomorrow, Amy, so that I might explain things to Mrs Dale and apologise. I didn't mean to hurt her, truly I didn't. I just felt dreadfully sorry for her, and thought that I could cheer her up by visiting and pretending to be you. I should have thought it through more carefully. If I had I wouldn't have been so stupid, and would have said no to the whole crazy idea!'

Amy, whose mind was reeling, said nothing, but the others believed Freddie at once. She had acted rashly, foolishly and thoughtlessly, but her heart had been in the right place. It was different with June, though, who was now sitting alone in the corner, keeping unusually quiet and looking rather ashamed of herself. And well she might, thought Felicity, who felt quite disgusted with the girl. The whole idea had been June's, and Felicity knew that she hadn't acted from motives of kindness. No, June's twisted sense of mischief had been at work, and she had certainly meant to cause trouble for Freddie. Felicity wondered why, as she and Freddie were supposed to be friends. But then June had always had a rather odd sense of humour!

'Will you have to report this to Miss Grayling?' Freddie asked Felicity now, looking rather scared. June's heart sank as she heard this. It had never even occurred to her that the Head might become involved, and June knew that Miss Grayling would not go easy on her. She might even expel her, and June felt sick at heart at the thought.

'That's for Amy to decide,' answered Felicity, looking across at the girl.

'I don't know,' said Amy, on whose face the strain was beginning to show. 'I just can't think about that at the moment. All I want is to meet my grandmother and get to know her. Freddie, you can come with me tomorrow. And I can let her know that she has been wrong about my father, and that he would like to meet her as well.'

'No!' cried Felicity and Freddie together.

'Amy, you can't,' said Felicity. 'Your grandmother would be terribly hurt if she knew how your mother had behaved. And she's going to have quite enough shocks to deal with tomorrow as it is. I'm afraid that your poor father is going to have to remain the villain of the piece for the time being.'

'Of course,' said Amy, running a hand over her brow. 'I'm not thinking very clearly.'

'Well, I'm sure it's no wonder,' said Pam, getting up as the bell for bedtime sounded. 'You've had an awful lot to take in tonight. Now it's time for bed, and you'll feel much better after a good night's sleep.'

But the following morning, neither Amy nor June looked as if they had slept very well, both of them pale and heavy-eyed. Amy had had far too much going on in her mind to allow her to sleep properly, while June knew that she was going to be in disgrace with the rest of her form, and – even worse – perhaps with Miss Grayling as well. No one spoke to her as she dressed and ate her breakfast, not even Freddie, and the silence was very hard to bear. Felicity sought her out after breakfast, and led her to one of the little music-rooms.

'I suppose you're going to tell me off,' said June, folding her arms across her chest, defiant to the last, even though she knew that she richly deserved a scolding.

'Yes, I am,' said Felicity bluntly. 'June, what were you thinking of? How could you have been so stupid and so cruel?'

'I admit that it was stupid,' said June. 'But I didn't intend to cause Mrs Dale any hurt.'

'Perhaps not,' said Felicity. 'But you certainly meant to cause trouble for Freddie. Why, June, when she's your friend and has never shown you anything but kindness?'

June turned red, but stubbornly refused to answer, while Felicity wracked her brains for a clue that might explain the girl's extraordinary behaviour. Then, in a flash, it came to her.

'*I* know why!' exclaimed Felicity. 'You're jealous of Freddie, of how clever she is at jokes and tricks. Because you desperately want to be the third form's bad girl, the only who can play tricks and make people laugh. Well, June, you've certainly proved that you're a bad girl – but no one's laughing.'

June was now as white as she had been red, and she said harshly, 'Very clever of you, Felicity. Have you finished now?'

'Not quite,' said Felicity. 'We have yet to hear you offer an apology to Amy, or Mrs Dale, or Freddie for what you've done. And you must see that you owe them one, all three of them.'

'I know that!' said June, growing angry. 'And I *shall* apologise to them, in my own time and without any prompting from you, Felicity.'

'I'm glad to hear it,' said Felicity. 'And for your sake, June, I hope that Amy decides not to report the matter to Miss Grayling. I wouldn't want to be in your shoes if she does!'

June went away smarting. She always hated to be told off, and Felicity had made her feel very small indeed.

Freddie, meanwhile, wasn't looking forward to seeing Mrs Dale at all. She and Amy made their way to her cottage after afternoon school, and were silent on the short walk, each girl lost in her own thoughts. As the little cottage came into sight, Freddie's footsteps seemed to drag, as though she were trying to put off the dreadful moment when she would have to confess everything to the old lady. But then they were at the gate, and Freddie turned to Amy. 'We're here.'

Mrs Dale springs a surprise

'Why, I wasn't expecting to see you until Sunday!' exclaimed Mrs Dale, as she opened the door to the two girls. 'And you've brought someone else to visit me. Come along in, both of you.'

She led both girls into her tiny living-room, where they sat side by side on a small sofa. Mrs Dale's cat, Sooty, who had become firm friends with Freddie, jumped up on to her knee and rubbed his head against her arm, purring madly. Then he spotted Amy, and wondered if this stranger liked cats too. Sooty jumped from Freddie's lap to Amy's, and the girl gave a little start, for she wasn't used to pets and was rather nervous of them. But Sooty was prepared to overlook this, and curled up on her lap, purring his approval when Amy tentatively stroked his head.

'Well, Amy,' said Mrs Dale, now that Sooty had settled down to his satisfaction. 'This is an unexpected pleasure.'

'Yes,' began Freddie. 'You see, I had to come today, because –'

'Oh, I wasn't talking to you, my dear,' said Mrs Dale, with a strange little smile. 'I was talking to my grand-daughter, Amy.'

Then she looked directly at Amy, whose mouth had

144

fallen open in shock, and said, 'That is who you are, isn't it?'

'Yes, Grandmother,' answered Amy in a trembling voice. 'Oh, it's so lovely to meet you!' Then she got to her feet, dislodging the cat – who merely yawned and settled down on Freddie again – and hugged the old lady for all she was worth, while Freddie looked on in the utmost astonishment, questions crowding her brain.

At last Amy and Mrs Dale sat back down again, and Freddie said, in rather a high, nervous voice, 'How long have you known that I wasn't Amy?'

'I've known from the first,' answered the old lady quite serenely, her shrewd eyes twinkling. 'I might be old, but I still have all my wits about me! You see, a couple of days before you turned up on my doorstep claiming to be my granddaughter, I received a letter from Amy's mother. And in it was a recent photograph of Amy, in her new school uniform, taken just before she left for Malory Towers.'

'But – but why didn't you say anything?' asked the bewildered Freddie, absent-mindedly stroking the cat.

'Because I wanted to know what game you were playing,' Mrs Dale replied. 'I was at a loss at first, but I think I know what you were up to now. I realised the other day, when you brought June to tea. She was the one who put you up to it, wasn't she?'

Amy gave a scornful snort, while Freddie nodded and said, 'Yes, but you must believe that I didn't mean any harm, Mrs Dale. June said that you were lonely, and it seemed like a good idea at the time, but . . .'

Her voice trailed off miserably and Mrs Dale said, 'But your conscience started to trouble you.'

'Yes, it did,' said Freddie, looking the old lady straight in the eye. 'It troubled me a lot. And there was something else too. I grew very fond of you – and I hadn't expected that.'

'Well, I'm glad to hear it,' said Mrs Dale, her shrewd blue eyes twinkling. 'Because I grew very fond of you, too, and came to look forward to your visits, even though I knew you weren't really my granddaughter. Heavens!' She gave a little laugh. 'Do you realise that I don't even know what your real name is?'

'I'm Freddie,' the girl answered. 'And I'm so relieved that you aren't angry with me.'

'I could tell that you were a good girl at heart,' said Mrs Dale. 'And I knew that you would own up sooner or later. As for that June – well, I realised that she was a monkey the second I clapped eyes on her. That was the day she rescued my Sooty from the tree. My goodness, what a long time ago that seems now!'

'Monkey is putting it mildly!' said Freddie, with a grimace. 'I was an idiot to let her talk me into this in the first place.'

'Oh, we all act foolishly at times,' said Mrs Dale. 'I just hope June comes to see the error of her ways before she gets herself into real trouble. She reminds me very much of myself when I was that age, you know.'

Both girls looked astonished at this, quite unable to picture the old lady as a mischievous schoolgirl, and Mrs

Dale laughed at their wide-eyed expressions. 'Yes, I was young once myself,' she said. 'And now, Freddie, I'm going to ask you to leave Amy and me alone for a while. I'd like to get to know my granddaughter.'

'Of course,' said Freddie, getting up at once and putting Sooty, who didn't approve of all this activity, on the floor. 'May I come and visit you again, please, Mrs Dale?'

'I should like that very much,' said the old lady with a smile. 'Only next time come as Freddie, not as Amy. And send June to see me as well. I'd like a word with that young lady!'

Freddie felt as if the weight of the world had rolled off her shoulders as she made her way back to Malory Towers, and there was a spring in her step when she walked into the common-room. June was there alone, and she looked up as Freddie entered. It was a lovely, crisp, sunny day outside and the rest of the third form were making the most of it by getting some fresh air. But nobody had asked June if she wanted to go with them. Not that she cared tuppence, for she would much rather be on her own than with a group of girls whose disgust and disapproval of her was all too plain. There was a moment's awkward silence, then Freddie, who felt so happy that she could almost forgive June, cleared her throat and asked, 'Where is everyone?'

'They're all outside,' answered June, heartened by the fact that Freddie had broken the ice between them. There was another pause and then she asked, 'Er – how did it go at Mrs Dale's? Was she very angry with you?'

'No, surprisingly enough, she wasn't,' said Freddie and, unable to keep it to herself any longer, she launched into her tale. June was astonished, of course, and asked a great many questions, feeling quite as relieved as Freddie that everything was all right.

'Of course, Amy will still have to tackle her mother,' said Freddie, when she reached the end of her story. 'Can you believe that anyone would be so stuck-up and snobbish as to be ashamed of her own mother? Honestly, June, doesn't it make you feel grateful that we have ordinary, sensible parents?'

June agreed heartily with this, then, after a moment's silence, said in a rush, 'Freddie, I'm sorry. I placed you in a very uncomfortable situation, and one that could have got you into a lot of trouble. I hope that you'll accept my apology, and that the two of us can still be friends. Though if you don't want to, I won't blame you.'

'I *would* like us to carry on being friends, June,' answered Freddie, her expression quite serious. 'But first I must know *why* you put me up to impersonating Amy. Because I know that it wasn't concern for Mrs Dale that made you do it.'

'You're right,' said June, realising that she would have to be completely honest with Freddie if their friendship was ever to get back on its old footing. So she told Freddie the truth – how she had begun to feel jealous of her, and hadn't wanted Freddie sharing in the adulation and glory June received from the others for her tricks. And how petty and spiteful it sounded when she said it aloud! No wonder Freddie looked shocked, and June wouldn't blame the girl if she decided that she didn't want to be her friend after all. But Freddie said, 'Thank you for having the courage to be honest with me, June. And if we are to remain friends, you must go on being honest. Even if it means telling me things that I don't want to hear sometimes.'

June nodded solemnly. 'I will,' she said. 'And you must try to be a steadying influence on me, and try to talk me out of some of the crazy ideas I come up with.'

'I'll do my best,' said Freddie, with a grin. 'But I doubt if *anyone* could stop you once you've taken it into your head to carry out one of your madcap schemes!'

So, when the rest of the third form poured in, rosy-cheeked from their walk in the grounds, it was to find June and Freddie chatting together amicably. Some of them exchanged surprised glances but Felicity, who felt that there had been quite enough ill feeling in the third form recently, was pleased and, knowing that the others would follow her lead, said cheerily, 'Hallo, you two! I say, Freddie, where's Amy? Still at her grandmother's?'

And Freddie had to relate, once more, all that had happened at Mrs Dale's for the benefit of the rest of the third form.

'Well!' said Nora when she had finished. 'So the old lady knew all along that you weren't Amy. She tricked you far more successfully than you tricked her, Freddie.'

'Good for her!' laughed Julie.

'And you didn't have to go through the unpleasantness

of owning up after all,' said Susan. 'I'll bet that was a relief, Freddie.'

There was more good news when Amy came back, just in time for supper. Felicity had been a little afraid that Amy, once she got to know her grandmother, might not get on with her because she was not as grand as the rest of her family. But it was plain from the bright smile on the girl's face that she had had a very happy time with Mrs Dale, and was overjoyed to have met her at last. Amy also announced graciously that she was not going to report Freddie and June to Miss Grayling. Freddie, who guessed that she had Mrs Dale to thank for this, was extremely grateful, while June got up and said, 'Thank you, Amy. Freddie and I appreciate it. And I want you to know that I'm really very sorry for the part that I played in this business. It was completely my fault, and Freddie would never have thought of pretending to be you if I hadn't put the idea into her head.'

After only a slight hesitation, Amy took June's outstretched hand and shook it, while Felicity breathed a sigh of relief. June's frank, open apology had done much to lighten the mood of the third formers and they admired her for being brave enough to make it in front of them all. Perhaps, at last, things were beginning to settle down a bit.

But not everything was sorted out, of course. Bonnie and Veronica were still very cool towards Felicity, and towards one another, while Amy still flatly refused to make up with Bonnie. Felicity, who felt rather guilty about the rift between the two girls, tactfully broached the subject with Amy later that evening, suggesting that she and Bonnie clear the air between them, but she was brushed off.

'I know that you mean well, Felicity,' said Amy stiffly. 'But Bonnie deceived me. And, quite frankly, I've had enough of deceitful people to last me a lifetime!'

Felicity guessed, of course, that Amy was referring to her mother and said no more, deciding that it would be foolish to push the matter when the girl had so much on her mind.

And Bonnie herself went up to Amy in the dormitory, as the third formers got ready for bed. Bonnie had been deeply shocked at the way Amy had been kept apart from her grandmother, and the incident had made her think of her own doting grandparents, who had always played a large part in her life and whose spoiling she had rather taken for granted. She felt very sorry for Amy, who had missed out on her own grandmother's loving companionship for so many years. For probably the first time in her life, Bonnie genuinely wanted to be of help and comfort to someone else.

'Amy, I'm so pleased that your meeting with your grandmother went well today,' she said in her soft voice. 'Have you decided what you're going to say to your mother?'

But Amy merely looked at Bonnie coldly and said, 'Did Felicity tell you to come and speak to me?'

'Of course not!' said Bonnie, deeply offended. 'I'm just concerned for you, that's all.'

151

'Amy doesn't need your concern,' butted in Veronica, who had been hovering nearby, listening jealously. 'She knows that she can always rely on me in times of trouble.'

'I'm sure that Amy can speak for herself,' snapped Bonnie, giving Veronica a look of dislike. 'Amy, you might not be my friend any more, but I'm yours, whether you want me to be or not. And I shall be here if you need me.'

But Bonnie received no response other than a look of icy disdain so, rather despondently, she went off to her own bed, while Amy and Veronica each climbed into theirs.

'What *are* you going to do about your parents?' whispered Veronica to Amy. 'My word, your father's going to be simply furious with your mother when he finds out what has been going on all these years.'

'Yes, he is,' answered Amy in a low voice. 'But I'm afraid that can't be helped. Mummy has brought it all on herself. I've decided that I'm going to tackle her at the weekend, when she and Daddy come over for my birthday. Really, Veronica, I don't know how she can have imagined, even for a second, that Daddy would look down on Grandmother! He may be wealthy, but he's awfully kind-hearted, and would never disapprove of someone simply because they don't have very much money.'

'And what about you, Amy?' asked Veronica curiously. 'How do you feel about your gran?'

'Why, I love her, of course,' said Amy, sounding rather surprised at the question. 'I did from the moment I saw her. She is my grandmother, after all!'

'Of course,' said Veronica. 'But what I really meant was –'

She stopped suddenly, realising that the question she wanted to ask wasn't very tactful, and Amy gave a soft laugh, realising all at once what Veronica wanted to know.

'You mean do *I* look down on her because she isn't wealthy, don't you?' she said. 'Well, I don't, surprising as it may seem. I know that I'm stuck-up and snobbish, and all of the other things that people say about me – and I probably always will be. But somehow it's impossible to look down on someone you love.'

Veronica felt rather guilty on hearing this. Hadn't she looked down on her own parents and thought that they weren't good enough for her? Well, she had learned her lesson all right at half-term, and she understood exactly how Amy was feeling now. 'No,' she murmured. 'You're quite right, Amy. You can't look down on the people you love.'

Her voice was becoming drowsy and, beside her, Amy stifled a yawn.

'No more talking now, girls,' came Felicity's voice. 'It's time for lights-out.'

And, one by one, the third formers drifted off to sleep, each of them thinking that the last few days had been very strange indeed, and wondering what the remainder of the term had in store.

A bad time for Felicity

The following day started badly for Felicity, who was putting her shoes and socks on when the breakfast bell went, only to discover that one of her laces was missing.

'What *are* you doing, Felicity?' asked Nora, astonished to see the girl dive under the bed in search of her missing shoelace.

'One of my laces is missing,' came Felicity's muffled voice from under the bed. 'Blow! Where *can* it have gone? I know they were both here last night.'

'It must have fallen out,' said Julie.

'Laces don't just *fall* out,' said Felicity, who was now crawling round the floor. 'And they don't simply disappear into thin air either. I can't go down to breakfast without it, or I shan't be able to keep my shoe on.'

'I've got a spare pair of shoelaces,' said Susan, coming to the rescue. 'You can borrow one of them. Now do hurry up, Felicity, or you'll get into a row from Potty.'

Quickly Felicity threaded the new lace into her shoe and raced downstairs after the others, reaching the dining-room just in time to avoid a ticking off from Miss Potts.

'I can't think where my shoelace went,' said Felicity to Susan as she buttered a slice of toast.

'Well, I shouldn't worry about it too much,' said Susan. 'It's not as if you've lost something valuable, like jewellery or your purse. Perhaps someone removed it while you were asleep, for a prank. I daresay it'll turn up later.'

Felicity decided that Susan was probably right and thought no more about the matter – at first.

June's mind seemed to be somewhere else at breakfast. Indeed, she was so preoccupied that she would have put salt in her porridge instead of sugar, if Freddie hadn't been on hand to stop her.

'Whatever is the matter with you?' asked Freddie. 'You've been in an absolute dream since you got out of bed!'

'I've just been thinking,' answered June. 'I've apologised to you, and I've apologised to Amy. Now all I need to do is square things with Mrs Dale, and once I've done that I'll feel as if I can wipe the slate clean.'

'Yes, I think you should get it over with as soon as possible, then you'll feel much better,' agreed Freddie. 'She's a decent old soul, and I don't think she'll be too cross with you – especially as you remind her of herself when she was young.'

June laughed. 'I couldn't believe it when you told me that, and I still can't imagine dear, kindly Mrs Dale playing pranks on her teachers!' She sipped her tea and went on decisively, 'I'm going to slip across and see her in the lunch-break. If I run over there quickly as soon as I've eaten, I can be there and back again in time for English this afternoon.'

Freddie nodded in approval at this plan, while at the

other end of the table, Julie said, 'Felicity! Don't forget that you said you'd lend me your spare pen. Mine's broken and I shan't have time to go and buy a new one until the weekend.'

'Oh yes, I *had* forgotten!' exclaimed Felicity. 'It's in the common-room. I'll go and fetch it on the way to Maths.'

But when Felicity and her friends popped into the common-room a little later, her spare pen was nowhere to be seen.

'That's strange!' said Susan, looking baffled. 'I could have sworn that you put it in your locker last night.'

'Yes, so could I,' said Felicity, frowning. 'Half a minute, though! Nora, I lent it to you, remember, because you had left yours in your desk. You're so scatterbrained that you must have forgotten to give it back to me.'

'I *did* give it back to you, Felicity,' insisted Nora. 'I'm sure I did.'

'Yes, she did,' put in Pam. 'I remember seeing her hand it to you. But goodness knows where you put it. Really, Felicity, first you lose your shoelace then you misplace your pen! You're getting quite as scatterbrained as Nora.'

But Felicity wasn't at all scatterbrained, and had been brought up to take care of her things. It wasn't like her at all to lose something, or to forget where she had put it, and she began to feel a little worried.

'Well, we can't stay here all morning hunting for a pen,' said Susan briskly. 'I don't think that Miss Peters would think that an acceptable excuse for us being late.

Julie, you'll have to see if one of the others has a pen you can borrow.'

So the girls quickly made their way to the third-form classroom, where, fortunately for Julie, she was able to borrow a pen from one of the South Tower girls. Miss Peters did not look at all kindly on girls who turned up to her classes badly prepared and without the correct equipment!

Felicity, however, continued to puzzle over her missing belongings. It wasn't as if they were expensive possessions, or things that were particularly important to her, or items that couldn't be replaced. It was just so very *annoying*!

True to her word, June sped across to Mrs Dale's cottage after lunch, and Freddie was waiting for her by the school gates when she returned, relieved to see the happy smile on the girl's face.

'Mrs Dale is the nicest, most decent person I have ever met!' she declared. 'Of course, she gave me a bit of a ticking off, but that was only to be expected. Then she started telling me about some of the tricks she had played when she was at school, and I told her about the vanishing cream, and we got along like a house on fire! She's given me some simply super ideas for tricks as well.'

'Tell me about them later,' said Freddie, taking June's arm and walking briskly up the drive. 'If we're late for English we shall be in trouble with Miss Hibbert, and you don't want another ticking off.'

The two girls got to their classroom just before the English mistress and were spared a scolding, but alas for

Felicity, she very soon got into trouble with Miss Hibbert.

'We're going to carry on reading through the play that we started yesterday,' said the mistress, once the class was seated. 'Open your scripts at page three and . . . Felicity, please pay attention!'

Felicity, who had been rummaging around in her desk, hastily dropped the lid and said, 'I'm sorry, Miss Hibbert, but I can't seem to find my script.'

'Really, Felicity, as head of the form you're supposed to set an example to the others,' said Miss Hibbert, sounding exasperated. 'It's most unlike you to be so careless. Well, you will just have to share Susan's script for now.'

Her face flaming, Felicity moved her chair closer to Susan's, as her thoughts raced. She had put the script back in her desk after English yesterday, she was absolutely certain of that! To mislay one thing might be put down to carelessness or absent-mindedness, but this was the third thing that she had lost today. An unwelcome suspicion entered Felicity's head. Was someone playing a prank on her? If so, it wasn't a very funny one, for it had got her into hot water with Miss Hibbert. Her heart sank as it occurred to her that, perhaps, the culprit meant for her to get into trouble, and she glanced round at the other girls in her form, wondering which of them could be capable of such spite. She was certain that it *was* a third former, for nobody else could have sneaked into the classroom and the dormitory and the common-room without being spotted. But there was no time to think about that now, for Felicity had to give her full attention to Miss Hibbert and the reading of the play.

She voiced her suspicions to Susan later that afternoon, as the two of them sat on a wooden bench in the courtyard, and her friend looked very serious indeed.

'I must admit that thought occurred to me too,' said Susan. 'But who on earth could it be? Not Pam, or Nora or Julie, that much is certain.'

'No, we can certainly rule them out,' said Felicity. 'We've known them since we were first formers together and none of them would think of doing anything so beastly to me. I don't think it's the kind of thing Freddie would do either. There's no shortage of suspects, though. I've upset Bonnie, Amy and Veronica recently – though Amy does seem to have got over it, and I honestly think she has too much on her mind at the moment to bother about playing silly, spiteful little tricks on me.'

Susan agreed and said gravely, 'I hate to say this, Felicity, but there's someone else it could be.'

'Who?' asked Felicity in surprise.

'June,' answered Susan. 'Don't forget that you told her off over that business with Mrs Dale, and that won't have gone down well. If there's one thing that June hates it's being made to feel small. You can't deny that she has a malicious streak in her nature, and we all know that she can hold a grudge too!'

Everything that Susan said was true, but Felicity hated to think that June, who had also come up through the school with them, was capable of such spite against her, even though they hadn't always been the best of friends.

'No,' she said at last, shaking her head. 'I know that June was angry with me for giving her a scold, but she also knew that she deserved it. Besides, if she did have a grudge against me she would tell me so to my face – and probably in front of everyone too! No, this hole and corner stuff isn't like June at all.'

But Susan wasn't convinced. 'She has done this kind of thing before,' she said. 'Remember when we were in the first form and she sent those horrid anonymous notes to Moira?'

Felicity was silent. She had forgotten all about that! Moira had been a very unpopular and rather domineering fifth former who had got on the wrong side of June. And June had retaliated by sending the girl a series of unpleasant anonymous notes. But she had been found out, and it was only thanks to Moira's intervention that June hadn't been expelled.

'Yes, but she was only a first former then,' said Felicity at last, looking troubled. 'And almost being expelled really shook her up and taught her a lesson. Surely she wouldn't do anything like that again – would she?'

'I really don't know *what* to think,' said Susan, frowning. 'But perhaps we should tell Pam, Nora and Julie that we suspect someone is playing these mean tricks on you, then all of us can keep our eyes open and look out for anything suspicious.'

'Good idea,' said Felicity. 'Oh, Susan, I do hope that it isn't June! It's bad enough to think that there's someone in the third form who dislikes me enough to take my things and get me into trouble – but it's even worse to think that it could be someone that I've known for years!'

The two girls found Pam, Nora and Julie down at the stables, all of them fussing over Jack. To their astonishment, Bonnie was also there, feeding sugar to Miss Peters's big black horse, Midnight, and patting his sleek, dark neck. Felicity noticed that the girl looked a little nervous when Midnight whinnied, and she shied away from him when he tossed his big head.

'I didn't know that you liked horses, Bonnie!' said Susan, in surprise.

'There are a lot of things you don't know about me, Susan,' said Bonnie, rather loftily. Then she gave Midnight a final pat and whispered to him, 'I'll be back to see you tomorrow, boy,' before walking out of the stables, pointedly sticking her nose in the air as she passed Felicity.

'I'd love to know what she's playing at,' said Nora, staring suspiciously after her. 'Julie says that Bonnie has been to see Midnight every day this week, yet she's never shown any interest in him – or any of the horses – before.'

'She's a funny little thing,' remarked Pam. 'I don't quite know what to make of her!'

'Well, never mind that now,' said Felicity. 'Susan and I have something we want to tell you.'

And Pam, Nora and Julie listened open-mouthed as the two girls told them that they were certain someone was playing malicious tricks on Felicity.

161

'I believe you're right!' said Pam. 'It's not like you to be careless with your belongings, Felicity.'

'I'll bet it's Veronica!' Nora said. 'You know that she did something very similar to Katherine of the fourth form, of course?'

'No, I didn't know!' said Felicity, looking shocked. 'When was this?'

'It was when they were in the second form together,' said Nora. 'Apparently the two of them fell out over something – I can't remember what – and strange things started happening to Katherine, just as they have to you, Felicity. Her things went missing, and some of her work was deliberately spoilt, and eventually Katherine and some of her friends caught Veronica red-handed. That's why the fourth formers always disliked Veronica so much, and, if you ask me, it's why Miss Grayling decided to keep her down with us instead of going up into the fourth form this term. I think she wanted Veronica to have a fresh start with a new form.'

'And instead it looks as if she's been up to her old tricks again,' said Julie, looking quite disgusted. 'How jolly mean of her, especially as you were so kind to her at half-term, Felicity.'

'Let's find her and have it out with her!' cried Susan, indignant on her friend's behalf.

But Felicity said decisively, 'No, we can't. We don't have any proof that it's Veronica who is behind this, and it would be a dreadful thing if we accused her wrongly.'

'You're quite right, old thing,' said Pam. 'None of us like

Veronica, but just because she's done this kind of thing before doesn't mean that she is responsible this time.'

'Well, I'm going to be watching her,' said Susan. 'And if I catch her in the act she had better watch out!'

'Yes, but don't let her know that you're watching her,' warned Julie. 'If it is Veronica, we don't want to put her on her guard.'

There was quite a lot of spying going on in the third form over the next couple of days. Susan, of course, was watching Veronica. Felicity, meanwhile, kept an eye on June, for of all the girls she suspected, June was the one she desperately hoped was innocent. And Nora and Julie were watching Bonnie – not because they thought that she was the person playing tricks on Felicity, for both of them privately thought that Veronica was responsible – but they were extremely curious to know what was behind the girl's sudden interest in Midnight.

They found out on Saturday morning, when they were busy grooming Jack. Miss Peters came into the stables to saddle up Midnight, only to find Bonnie there petting him and feeding him a carrot. Midnight had grown very fond of Bonnie, and would whinny softly when she approached him, before nuzzling her shoulder. Bonnie, in turn, had quite lost her fear of the big horse and thought him rather sweet. He swallowed the last bit of carrot now and rested his black head on Bonnie's shoulder, while she threw her arms round his neck and said in her lisping voice, 'Dear Midnight, what a lovely horse you are! Miss Peters is so lucky to have you.'

'Why, Bonnie!' cried Miss Peters, coming up behind the girl. 'I had no idea that you and Midnight were such good friends.'

'Oh, Miss Peters, I didn't hear you come in!' said Bonnie, turning her big brown eyes on the mistress. 'Yes, I absolutely adore Midnight, though I must admit I was a little afraid of horses until I got to know him. But he's so sweet and gentle that now I can't believe what a silly I was!'

And, under the astonished eyes of Julie and Nora, Miss Peters – who loved Midnight more than anything or anyone else in the world – beamed at Bonnie and said kindly, 'I'm glad that he has helped you to overcome your fear. Perhaps you would like me to take you out on him one day, Bonnie? I can lead him while you sit on his back and just get used to being on a horse.'

'Oh, Miss Peters!' cried Bonnie ecstatically, her eyes shining. 'That would be simply marvellous.'

'Very well,' said the mistress, putting the saddle on to the horse's back. 'I can't take you out now, for I've arranged to meet Bill and Clarissa, but perhaps one day next week?'

Bonnie thanked Miss Peters again, and waved her off as she led Midnight out into the yard before nimbly mounting him and riding off. Then, as the clip-clop of the horse's hooves faded into the distance, she turned to the two third formers and said sweetly, 'Looks like you owe me a stick of toffee, Nora.'

And Nora had to laugh. Bonnie was quite a determined little character once she had made up her mind to do something, even overcoming her fear of horses because she knew that Miss Peters was sure to look kindly on anyone who liked her beloved Midnight. She really was the strangest girl!

15

Veronica in trouble

The following day, Sunday, was Amy's birthday and the girl had been looking forward to it with mixed feelings. The excitement she would normally have felt was dimmed, because she knew that she would have to tackle her mother about the lies she had told. All the same, it was pleasant to wake up to a chorus of 'Happy Birthday' from the third formers, and – as she knew that she wasn't the most popular girl in the form – Amy was both amazed and delighted to find that everyone had bought her a gift. They were only small things – a jar of bath salts from Veronica, chocolate from Felicity and a hair-slide from Pam, but Amy thanked everyone and smiled round pleasantly. She went into the bathroom to wash, and when she came back there was a large parcel on her bed, wrapped in silver paper with a bow on top. Curious, she ripped it open and gave a gasp. For there was the dress that Bonnie had promised her. The two girls had chosen the material together before they quarrelled, and Amy had assumed that Bonnie was no longer going to make the dress. But here it was, and what a super job Bonnie had done! Amy's eyes shone as she held the pale pink dress against her and Nora said, 'My word, Amy, that's simply beautiful! Is that Bonnie's work?'

'Yes, it is,' answered Amy, glancing across at Bonnie, who was sitting on her bed, bending over to tie her shoelaces, apparently unconcerned, but inwardly hoping that her generous gesture would mend the rift between herself and Amy. And it seemed that it had done the trick, for Amy walked across to Bonnie and, a little awkwardly, said, 'Thank you, Bonnie. That was very kind and thoughtful of you.'

Bonnie looked up and said, 'I'm glad you like it.'

'I like it very much,' said Amy. 'You must have worked like a Trojan to get it finished in time for my birthday. I shall wear it today.'

Immensely gratified, Bonnie smiled. Then she became serious again and said, 'Amy, please can we be friends again? I've missed you so much and I promise that I'll be a *true* friend to you from now on.'

And Amy, who was becoming a little tired of Veronica's company, and missed having someone to chat to about hair-dos and clothes, agreed. Of course, Veronica was not at all pleased that the two girls had made up their quarrel, for she had enjoyed having Amy to herself and now it seemed that she would have to vie with Bonnie for her attention again.

Amy's parents came to collect her at lunchtime and, as the girl got ready to go down and greet them, Felicity said to her, 'I do hope that all goes well for you, Amy, and that your father isn't too angry and upset with your mother. We shall be thinking of you.'

And the third formers did think of her, often, that day,

for although Amy hadn't done much to endear herself to them, they were good-hearted girls and wished her well.

But Felicity had problems of her own to think about, for her belongings were still going missing, and she and her friends were no nearer to finding out who the culprit was. Only yesterday, she had discovered her hairbrush had gone, and she had to borrow Susan's. Really, she thought, it was stealing, but the things the thief was taking were items that were of no value at all. What good was one shoelace, or a script for a play?

Only this morning she had said to Susan, 'I don't understand. Why doesn't she help herself to my purse, or the watch that my parents gave me for my birthday?'

'I think I understand,' said Susan, who had been giving the matter a lot of thought. 'Whoever it is doesn't want these things for herself, she's taking them to annoy you.'

'Well, she's certainly succeeding!' said Felicity. 'But she's going to have to stop soon or I shall have nothing left for her to take!'

Well, there was no point sitting around brooding about it, she decided now. Amanda was holding a lacrosse practice shortly, so she might as well go along to that. Susan had mentioned that she would like to go as well, so Felicity sped off to find her. Susan wasn't in the common-room, so Felicity went up to the dormitory to see if she was there. But as she approached, Felicity heard the sound of raised, angry voices coming from inside. Cautiously, she pushed open the door, and frowned as she realised that the two girls who were rowing were Susan and Veronica! Veronica looked upset and tearful, while Susan was obviously very angry indeed. And on the floor between them was the photograph of herself, Darrell and their parents that Felicity kept on her cabinet, its glass shattered.

'My photograph!' she gasped. 'What happened?'

'You had better ask dear Veronica,' said Susan in a hard voice. 'She can probably tell you where your missing things are as well.'

'No!' cried Veronica. 'I bumped into your cabinet, Felicity, and the photograph fell off and smashed. Susan came in and saw me bending over it, and jumped to conclusions.'

'But what were you doing near my cabinet anyway?' asked Felicity suspiciously. 'Your bed is at the other end of the room, so you had no reason to be over here at all.'

'I – I was looking out of the window,' stammered Veronica.

'What a lame excuse!' said Susan scornfully. 'We might be more inclined to believe you, Veronica, if we didn't know that you had done this kind of thing before.'

Veronica turned white and Susan went on, 'We know that you played mean tricks on Katherine, when both of you were in the second form. And now you're doing exactly the same to Felicity.'

'I admit that I was mean to Katherine,' said Veronica with a sob. 'And the rest of the form never forgave me, no matter how hard I tried to show that I was sorry. In the end I decided it wasn't worth being nice to them, and turned into the sly, sneaky creature they had already decided I was. But I *haven't* played tricks on Felicity!'

'I don't believe you,' said Susan, a disgusted expression on her face. 'You were caught out and now you're trying to talk your way out of it. Why can't you have the decency to own up and give Felicity her things back?'

'Because I don't have them!' yelled Veronica, tears running down her cheeks now. 'Felicity, you must believe me.'

'Veronica, I need to think about all this,' said Felicity, hardly able to look at the girl. She felt quite certain that Veronica was guilty, but at the same time she couldn't help feeling a little sorry for the girl.

'Come on, Susan,' she said at last. 'We'll be late for lacrosse practice if we don't hurry.'

Not that Felicity's mind was on lacrosse at all. She was quite unable to concentrate and didn't play up to her usual standard at all, which earned her a few sharp words from Amanda.

'Never mind, old thing,' said Susan, as they made their way to the changing-room afterwards.

'But I *do* mind!' said Felicity crossly. 'Blow Veronica! Not only has she been plaguing me with these spiteful tricks, but she's probably ruined my chances of getting into one of the teams this term as well!'

'Are you going to go to the Head about her?' asked Susan.

'I don't know,' sighed Felicity. 'As this is the second time she's done something like this, Miss Grayling will probably come down pretty hard on her. She might even expel her!'

'Well, it's quite her own fault,' said Susan unsympathetically. 'She simply can't go around behaving like that and expect to get away with it.'

'I'll sleep on it, and decide whether or not to report her to the Head tomorrow,' decided Felicity. 'And I suppose we'd better let the others know that we've solved the mystery.'

Veronica didn't put in an appearance at teatime, and Mam'zelle Dupont frowned when she saw the two empty places at the table.

'Who is missing?' she asked. 'Ah yes, Amy is out with her parents, is she not? But where is Veronica?'

'I don't think she was feeling very well, Mam'zelle,' said Felicity uncomfortably, feeling that someone ought to make an excuse for Veronica's absence in case the French mistress decided to make enquiries.

'Ah, *la pauvre*!' said Mam'zelle sympathetically. 'If she feels no better tomorrow, she must go to Matron and have some medicine.'

'I don't think Matron has any medicine that will cure a guilty conscience,' muttered Susan under her breath to Felicity. 'This proves that she's the one who was playing tricks on you, for she's afraid to come and face us.'

'What *are* you talking about?' asked Pam, who was on Susan's other side and had overheard some of this.

'We'll tell you later,' said Felicity in a low voice, leaning across. 'You, Nora and Julie come to the little music-room after tea. I don't want old Mam'zelle listening in.'

So, as soon as tea was over, the five girls rushed off to the music-room, and there was an outcry when Pam, Nora and Julie heard that it was Veronica who had been behind Felicity's troubles.

'The mean beast!'

'I *knew* it was her! A leopard never changes its spots.'

'And to think that she didn't even have the courage to own up when she was caught in the act!'

'My word, won't I tell her what I think of her when I see her!' said Julie angrily.

But Felicity said, 'Please don't say anything to her tonight, Julie. I need to think about whether I'm going to tell the Head or not. Besides, I should think that Amy has had quite a trying day, and I don't want her walking into a bad atmosphere when she comes back.'

'It's jolly decent of you to feel like that and to put Amy first,' said Pam warmly. 'But I suppose that's what makes you such a good head-girl.'

Felicity turned quite pink with pleasure and said, 'Do you *really* think that I'm a good head-girl?'

'I think you're first class,' said Pam firmly. 'You always consider other people's feelings, you're kind and helpful – and you're not domineering.'

'Hear, hear!' chorused the others.

'Thank you!' laughed Felicity, feeling very pleased indeed. 'Now we'd better go to the common-room, before the others send out a search party.'

'I wonder if Veronica will be there,' said Nora.

'Don't worry, Felicity, I shan't say anything to her, or to the others – yet.'

Veronica *was* in the common-room, looking very pale and red-eyed – and so was Amy. She was telling Bonnie and Veronica about her day, and the others gathered round to listen.

'Mummy didn't even attempt to make any excuses for herself, once she knew that I had met Grandmother,' Amy was saying. 'She said that she had intended to tell Daddy the truth once they were married, but that somehow the longer she put it off the harder it got.'

'Well, I can sort of understand that,' said Freddie. 'Was your father simply furious?'

'He was, rather,' said Amy, with a grimace. 'And terribly hurt that Mummy thought he wouldn't want to marry her simply because her parents hadn't been wealthy. He had come round a bit by the time I said goodbye to them though. He simply adores Mummy, you see, and he can never stay cross with her for very long. And meeting Grandmother helped. We went there after lunch, and she and Daddy are firm friends now.'

'That is good news!' said Felicity, happily. 'But how did you explain your father's rather sudden change of heart?'

'Well, we couldn't tell her the truth, of course, for it would have hurt her too much,' said Amy. 'So we just said that Mummy and I had talked him round and he realised how foolish and snobbish he had been. Poor Daddy had to apologise to Grandmother and, I must say, he did it very convincingly. I never realised that he was such a good actor! And the best thing of all is that Daddy is going to find Grandmother a little house near ours, so I shall be able to see her in the holidays.'

'That must have been the best birthday present of all!' cried Susan, marvelling at how happy Amy looked.

'Yes, it was,' agreed Amy. 'Oh, and Grandmother baked me the most *enormous* birthday cake, to bring back to school with me. We'll all share it at teatime tomorrow.'

The third formers rubbed their hands together at this, and there were cries of 'Jolly decent of you, Amy!'

Then Freddie, who had been looking rather wistful, sighed and said, 'I shall miss Mrs Dale awfully. I do think you're lucky to have her as a gran, Amy.'

'Well, she'll be here until the end of term,' said Amy. 'And I know that she'd like you to visit her again before she leaves, Freddie.'

That cheered Freddie up, and it was a happy bunch of third formers who trooped up to bed a little later. Apart from two of them. Felicity had been surreptitiously watching Veronica while they were in the common-room, and the girl had looked thoroughly miserable, lost in her own thoughts and hardly uttering a word. And Felicity herself, of course, was deeply troubled, as she knew that she would soon have to make a decision about whether or not to report Veronica to the Head. If only it was clear cut, but when the girl had been talking of her troubles with Katherine earlier, and of how her form had snubbed her efforts to make amends, Felicity had caught a glimpse of that humbler, softer Veronica that she had seen at half-term. The decision that Felicity made would affect Veronica's whole future, and the girl felt the responsibility weighing heavily on her slim shoulders.

At last Felicity fell asleep, and when she awoke her mind was clear. If Veronica went unpunished, and thought that she had got away with her mean tricks, it could lead her into far more serious trouble.

She signalled to Susan, Pam, Julie and Nora to stay behind in the dormitory as the others went down to breakfast, and told them of her decision.

'I really do think that you have made the right decision, Felicity,' said Susan. 'And I only hope that Veronica learns something from all this. When are you going to see Miss Grayling?'

'I'll go right after breakfast,' said Felicity. 'It's not going to be pleasant, and I'd rather get it over with as soon as possible.'

'I know that Veronica's behaviour has been despicable,' said Pam, with a frown. 'But I hope that Miss Grayling doesn't expel her.'

Suddenly a little squeal sounded from behind the group of girls and they all turned sharply, to see Bonnie standing there, a startled look on her face.

'Bonnie!' cried Felicity. 'I thought that you had gone to breakfast.'

'I was in the bathroom,' said Bonnie, an odd expression on her face. 'Pam, why should Miss Grayling expel Veronica?'

Pam exchanged a look with Felicity, who nodded and

said, 'There's no reason why you shouldn't tell Bonnie the truth. Everyone will know soon enough.'

'Well, Bonnie, we found out that Veronica was responsible for Felicity's things going missing,' Pam told the girl. 'Not only that, but she smashed her photograph.'

Bonnie said nothing, but just stood there looking absolutely stunned, and the girls, knowing that she was no friend of Veronica's, wondered why.

'I say, Bonnie, do you feel all right?' asked Julie.

'Yes, but I need to speak to Felicity privately,' said Bonnie, twisting her hands together agitatedly. 'Would the rest of you mind awfully leaving us alone?'

So, bursting with curiosity, the others went off to breakfast, while Felicity wondered what on earth Bonnie wanted. The girl hadn't spoken to her at all lately, unless she absolutely had to, so whatever she had to say must be extremely important.

Veronica gets a chance

'What is it, Bonnie?' asked Felicity, who was hungry and didn't want to get into trouble for being late in to breakfast.

Bonnie didn't answer. Instead, she went to the little cabinet beside her bed and pulled out a cardboard box, which she passed to Felicity.

'Take a look inside,' she said.

Felicity removed the lid – and gave a gasp. For there inside were her missing belongings. Her pen, the script of the play, a shoelace – and all the other things that she had mislaid recently.

'But I don't understand!' exclaimed Felicity, looking perplexed. 'How did they come to be in your cabinet, Bonnie? Did Veronica ask you to hide them for her?'

This seemed most unlikely, given that Bonnie and Veronica were hardly the best of friends, but Felicity could think of no other explanation.

'Of course not,' said Bonnie, gazing doe-eyed at Felicity. 'Veronica didn't take your things. It was me.'

'*You?*' said Felicity, sitting down plump upon her bed, so great was her astonishment. 'But – but why, Bonnie?'

'To pay you back for being mean to me, of course,' answered Bonnie simply, as though it was the most normal thing in the world for her to have played spiteful tricks on Felicity. 'You see, I thought you were my friend. And then, when I found out that you weren't, I was terribly angry. But, of course, I quite see that I couldn't let Veronica take the blame and possibly be expelled, much as I dislike her.'

Felicity was quite speechless for a moment, taken aback as much by Bonnie's matter-of-fact honesty as by the realisation that she was the person who had been playing pranks on her. At last she found her voice and said, 'Yes, it would have been very wrong of you to let Veronica take the blame. But, Bonnie, didn't it also occur to you that it was wrong to take my things in the first place? Why, it's stealing!'

'Of course it isn't!' said Bonnie. 'I never meant to keep your stuff. Why, what on earth would I want with an odd shoelace and a copy of a script that I already have? I always intended to give you your things back at the end of term. And I couldn't think of another way of getting back at you.'

Bonnie, thought Felicity, had a way of explaining the most extraordinary things so that they seemed quite ordinary! She tried once more to impress upon the girl that she had done wrong, saying, 'But you must have known that I was annoyed and upset about my things going missing?'

'Yes, I did,' said Bonnie, nodding her pretty head. 'But that was the whole point. I mean to say, what's the good of playing those kind of tricks on someone if it doesn't bother them?'

'Yes, but Bonnie, the thing is that you *shouldn't* have played those tricks on me at all,' said Felicity earnestly. 'I understand that you felt hurt, but that isn't the way that we deal with things at Malory Towers.'

'Really? Very well then, I shan't do it again,' said Bonnie blithely. 'Oh dear, Felicity, do look at the time! We shall get into a dreadful row if we go down to breakfast now. Not that I'm very hungry, are you?'

'Not any more,' answered Felicity, sighing. 'Bonnie, you do realise that I'm going to have to tell Susan and the others about this, don't you? Not to mention Veronica herself.'

'Must you?' said Bonnie, pouting a little. 'I was rather hoping that we could keep it just between the two of us.'

'Well, we can't,' said Felicity firmly. 'The others have a terrific down on Veronica because they think that she was behind all those tricks on me, and I must set them straight. And as for Veronica herself – my goodness, it must be simply dreadful to be wrongly accused of something when you know that you are innocent! I must tell her as soon as possible that her name has been cleared.'

'Yes, I suppose that you must do that,' agreed Bonnie, a little reluctantly. 'Though I suppose it means that everyone will turn against me now. How horrid!'

But somehow Felicity knew that Bonnie, who was a great deal tougher than she looked, would cope with the situation in her own way.

'The sly little beast!' cried Susan, when Felicity broke the news to her, Nora, Pam and Julie after morning school.

179

'That's the thing about Bonnie, though,' remarked Pam thoughtfully. 'Even when she's being sly, she's quite honest about it. I mean to say, she was going to own up to what she had done and give Felicity her things back all along. So really, she's *not* being sly.'

'She certainly has her own, unique way of looking at things,' said Nora, shaking her head. 'Although some of her ideas are quite wrong, of course.'

'I daresay some of our ways will rub off on her when she's been at Malory Towers for a while,' said Julie. 'That's the best of a splendid school like this – as well as learning things like Maths and English and all the rest of it, you learn other things that are equally important. Things like a sense of decency, fairness and responsibility.'

But Susan was less inclined to be lenient and, when the other three girls had departed, she said to Felicity, 'I hope that you are going to let Miss Grayling deal with Bonnie.'

'I hadn't really thought about it,' said Felicity, biting her lip. 'Do you think that I should, Susan?'

'Of course!' said Susan firmly. 'You were going to report Veronica to the Head, so I don't see what the difference is.'

'There *is* a difference,' said Felicity. 'Bonnie hasn't been to school before, and she doesn't fully understand –'

'Oh, Felicity, don't *you* start sticking up for her!' Susan interrupted impatiently. 'At her age she ought to know the difference between right and wrong. Not having been to school before can't be used as an excuse for simply *everything*, you know!'

Felicity knew that Susan was right. But she also knew

that Susan was angry at herself, as well as Bonnie, for she had been the first one to accuse Veronica directly of playing tricks on Felicity. So she slipped her arm through Susan's and said, 'Don't let's you and I fall out about this, old thing. That would be worse than anything! I'll think about reporting Bonnie, I promise. But before I do anything else, I must apologise to Veronica.'

Her anger cooling instantly, Susan gave Felicity's arm a squeeze and said ruefully, 'You're not the only one who owes Veronica an apology. I was very quick to accuse her, and didn't even bother listening to her explanation because I had made my mind up that she was guilty. This will certainly be a lesson to me not to judge people too hastily, I can tell you. Come along, let's go and find her now.'

Veronica was standing alone, glumly watching a group of second formers tossing a ball around, and both girls felt sorry for her. A thought occurred to Felicity and she said, 'I bet that Veronica's going to be pushed out, now that Amy and Bonnie have made up.'

Susan agreed and said, 'I never thought that Amy was very keen on Veronica anyway. The two of them have absolutely nothing in common. I can't say that I'm terribly fond of Veronica, but it must be simply dreadful having no one to talk to, or to share fun and secrets with. What a pity that we can't help her in some way.'

'But we can,' said Felicity, excitedly. 'You see, Susan, I think that there's another side to Veronica – a kind, decent side. I've seen it once or twice and I think that if we try hard – really hard – perhaps we can bring it out.'

Susan, eager to make up to Veronica for accusing her unjustly, said at once, 'What do you have in mind?'

'Well, I just think that we ought to give her a chance – you know, be nice to her and include her in things. Now that Amy isn't so eager for her company, I think she might take the chance that we are offering.'

'Yes, let's do that,' said Susan. 'Though I can think of one person who won't want any part of it – and that's June. She's never had any time for Veronica, and she's bound to pour cold water on the idea.'

'June can jolly well do as she's told and follow our lead for once,' retorted Felicity, a determined expression on her face. 'And if she dares to sneer at me I shall have a few words to say to her!'

And, looking at the glint in her friend's eye, Susan had no doubt that Felicity would do just that! But now they had another matter to deal with, and Felicity didn't beat around the bush, going across to Veronica and saying frankly, 'Veronica, I know now that it wasn't you who took my things and I'm sorry that I didn't believe you when you said that you were innocent. Please accept my apology.'

She held her hand out and Veronica, looking a little disbelieving at first, took it, and said, 'What's happened? Have you found out who really did it?'

'Yes,' said Felicity. 'It was Bonnie. She owned up when she found out that I suspected you.'

'And I'm sorry too, Veronica,' said Susan, coming forward. 'I saw you standing over the broken photograph and was ready to believe the worst of you. It was very wrong of me.'

Veronica, looking both surprised and pleased, turned red and said, 'No, it wasn't. It's quite my own fault if people think badly of me, I see that now. And I admit that I didn't like you very much at first, Felicity, but I could never do a mean act to someone who showed me the kindness that you and your parents did at half-term. No matter what happens between us in the future, that is something I shall never forget.'

Now it was Felicity's turn to go red, for she felt quite moved by Veronica's little speech – and there could be no doubting the girl's sincerity. Susan stepped into the breach, saying, 'Felicity and I were just off to lacrosse practice. Why don't you come along with us, Veronica?'

Amazed, and secretly delighted to be asked, Veronica said, 'There's no point in me coming. I'm not very good at lacrosse – or any games, for that matter.'

'Perhaps not, but you can still come along to watch, and shout a few words of encouragement to Susan and me,' said Felicity. 'Goodness knows we could do with them!'

So it came about that June and Freddie, who were already on the lacrosse field, were quite astonished to see Felicity, Susan and *Veronica*, of all people, coming towards them, all three girls chattering amicably together.

'Our dear Veronica seems to have made two new friends,' drawled June, once Veronica had taken her place on the sidelines and Felicity and Susan were on the field. 'Really, Felicity, I know that you always like to see the best in people, but surely even you must see that you're wasting your time with *her*.'

'You're wrong, June,' said Felicity, refusing to be ruffled by June's mocking tone. 'Susan and I have decided to give Veronica a chance to prove that she's not as bad as people think. And I would like the rest of the form, including *you*, June, to follow our lead.'

June laughed and said jeeringly, 'I'm not sucking up to that sly, spiteful beast. If you ask me –'

But June got no further, for Freddie piped up unexpectedly, giving June a push and saying sharply, 'No one did ask you, June! You ought to be the first to give Veronica a chance, considering the way you have behaved this term.'

'Freddie is quite right,' said Susan sternly. 'At least Veronica has learned something from her mistakes, but I don't think that you have, June.'

'Oh, June has nothing to learn,' said Felicity, giving the girl a hard look. 'She knows it all, don't you, June?'

Disconcerted by this sudden attack from all sides, June was lost for a suitable retort and Felicity went on, 'The trouble with you, June, is that nothing makes a lasting impression on you. I know that you regretted getting Freddie involved with Mrs Dale and were shaken by the upset you caused. And I'm willing to bet that you told Freddie – *and* yourself – that you had learned your lesson. But you haven't. Now that you've been forgiven by all concerned, you're back to your bold, bumptious, hard-hearted old self again.'

'Yes, and you promised me that you would do anything to make it up to me, if only I would forgive you,' said Freddie. 'Well, June, if you really mean that, I want you to back Felicity up and at least *try* to be nice to Veronica.'

June had to admit that there was a lot of truth in the others' words, and she certainly didn't want to fall out with Freddie again, so she said, 'I know that I can be hard, sometimes – it's just the way I am. My cousin Alicia was the same, though she softened a little as she got older, and perhaps I will too. As for being bumptious, Alicia used to say that I was like a rubber ball – no matter how hard anyone tried to squash me flat I always bounced back into shape again. Perhaps that will change one day, as well. And you're all absolutely right about one thing – I *have* behaved dreadfully this term and I *should* give Veronica a chance to prove that she has a good side. And that's exactly what I intend to do.'

That was good enough for Felicity. June had her faults – bad faults – but if she said she would do a thing she stuck to it.

Veronica was also doing her best, and surprised herself by becoming completely wrapped up in the practice game that took place, excitedly calling out her encouragement to the others.

'Play up, Susan!'

'Jolly good shot, Felicity!'

'Oh, well done, June!'

This last came as June took a particularly difficult shot at goal and managed to get the ball past the goalkeeper.

And Felicity was pleased when June heard Veronica's cry and turned to smile at her, giving her a cheery wave. With only one week to go to the end of term, perhaps things were finally sorting themselves out. Now, if only Felicity could decide what to do about Bonnie!

Felicity took a little time to herself after tea to walk alone in the grounds and consider the problem, but as dusk began to fall she was no nearer a solution. Bonnie certainly needed to be brought to a sense of her wrongdoing, and to learn that she couldn't take revenge every time someone upset her. She was spoilt, vain and quite unscrupulous when it came to getting her own way. But, Felicity had come to realise, the girl actually had quite a few good qualities too. She was single-minded and determined when she had a goal in sight, honest and not afraid to speak up for herself. And where better than Malory Towers for Bonnie to learn to cultivate these qualities and strive to make the good in her character cancel out the bad?

So lost in thought was she, that Felicity didn't realise she had walked as far as Miss Grayling's private garden, until the Head herself appeared in front of her.

'Why, it's you, Felicity!' she said in surprise. 'What are you doing over here, my dear?'

'I was thinking about something, Miss Grayling, and didn't realise that I had come so far,' said Felicity. 'I suppose that I had better make my way back to North Tower.'

Miss Grayling looked hard at the girl for a moment, then said, 'Actually, I'm glad you're here, for there's something I wanted to discuss with you. Come into my study.'

Felicity followed Miss Grayling across her neat little lawn, and through the French windows into her study, wondering what the Head wanted to talk to her about. Not more trouble, surely?

Miss Grayling took a seat behind her big desk and invited Felicity to sit opposite her, then she began, 'I wanted to speak to you about Veronica Sharpe. As you are probably aware, she wasn't very popular with her own form, which is why I decided to keep her back for a term, to see if a break from the girls who disliked her so much would do her good. As head-girl of the third form, I want to know what you think of her.'

'Well, we've had a few problems with Veronica,' said Felicity, feeling very honoured that the Head had asked her opinion and wanting to be as honest as possible. 'And she hasn't been awfully popular with our form either. But I think that, underneath it all, she's actually quite a decent person. We're all doing our best to give her a chance to prove herself, and she seems to be taking it.'

'That is good to hear,' said Miss Grayling. 'You see, Felicity, Veronica is really too old to stay down in the third form for more than a term. I have discussed the matter with Miss Peters and we both feel that Veronica ought to join the fourth formers next term. She will have had a long break from them, and they from her, so hopefully they will be able to start afresh.'

Felicity hoped so too. Perhaps she ought to have a talk with Katherine, who was now head-girl of the fourth, and see if she could persuade her to let bygones be bygones. If

Katherine was willing to hold out the hand of friendship to Veronica, the rest of the fourth formers were sure to do so as well. Then it occurred to Felicity that, if she was going to report Bonnie to the Head, now was as good a time as any. The trouble was, deep down inside, she *didn't* want to involve Miss Grayling, but would far rather keep what she had done a private third-form matter. Was it weakness on her part to feel like that? Felicity hoped not, for she so wanted to be a strong leader, like Darrell had been. As these thoughts flitted across the girl's mind, Miss Grayling's keen blue eyes watched her, seeing a lot more than Felicity realised. At last the Head asked, 'Is anything troubling you, Felicity?'

'Er – no, Miss Grayling, of course not,' she answered, nerves making her voice rather high.

'Are you sure?' asked Miss Grayling. 'You know that if you have any worries you can always bring them to me. That is what I am here for, after all.'

Felicity hesitated. Could she tell the Head what was on her mind without bringing Bonnie's name into it? She decided to try and began, 'Well, you see, Miss Grayling, I've had a problem with a girl in the third form. It's quite a trivial matter, and I think that I would rather deal with it myself than report it. But I can't be certain that I am doing the right thing, either for the form as a whole, or for the girl concerned. I keep asking myself what Darrell would have done in this situation, but –'

'My dear Felicity, what on earth does Darrell have to do with the matter?' the Head interrupted sharply.

'She was always so sure of herself,' said Felicity. 'And such a marvellous Head Girl. Somehow I feel that if I make the wrong decision, I will be letting her down as well as myself.'

'Darrell was an excellent Head Girl,' agreed Miss Grayling. 'But that isn't to say that she never made mistakes, particularly when she was lower down the school. Darrell wasn't perfect – nobody is. I recall that she had an extremely hot temper that caused her problems on a number of occasions!'

The Head smiled as she said this, and Felicity smiled shyly back, saying, 'She still *does* have a hot temper, though she has learned to control it a lot better now.'

'Exactly,' said Miss Grayling. 'She *learned* to control it. As you, Felicity, will learn to have faith in your own instincts and your own judgement. You see, Darrell isn't head of the third form – *you* are. And you are very different from Darrell, so you must stop wondering what she would do in this situation, or that situation. As for how you should deal with the matter you brought up – well, I think you have already answered that yourself. Do what *you* feel is right. It may turn out to be the wrong decision, but at least it will be *your* decision.'

And, as Felicity listened to Miss Grayling's words of wisdom, everything suddenly became crystal clear in her mind. She had worried too much about what other people thought of her, and about whether they were comparing her unfavourably to her older sister. Being a strong leader didn't always mean being outspoken, or forthright. It meant being true to yourself and your own character. And from now on, thought Felicity, as she said goodbye to the Head, that was exactly what she was going to be!

A happy end to the term

The last week of term simply flew by, and there was an air of great excitement throughout the school as the girls began to look forward to Christmas, pantomimes and parties.

'My first term as head of the form is almost over already,' said Felicity to Susan. 'And my word, what a term it's been!'

'It's certainly had its ups and downs,' agreed Susan. 'Thank goodness the last few days have been mostly ups!'

'Yes, Amy's been a lot happier since that business with her grandmother was settled,' said Felicity. 'And even Bonnie has been showing a bit of common sense since I gave her that talking to.'

Felicity, having decided that she wasn't going to report Bonnie for her bad behaviour, had taken the girl to one side to inform her of the fact. Bonnie, however, didn't seem to realise what a lucky escape she had had, merely smiling and saying off-handedly, 'Oh, thanks, Felicity,' before bending her head over the sewing she was working on. Felicity had stared down at the girl's curly head for a few moments, before coming to another decision. Bonnie might have been spared a dressing-down from Miss Grayling, but Felicity was jolly well

191

going to tell her what standard of behaviour was expected of a Malory Towers girl.

Bonnie listened open-mouthed and, when Felicity finished her stern little speech, she managed to squeeze out a few tears. Felicity, though, was quite convinced that they weren't genuine and were just an attempt to gain sympathy, so she remained quite unmoved by them. And, over the next few days, she noticed that Bonnie did seem to be making an effort to behave more sensibly, which pleased Felicity immensely and made her feel that her words hadn't fallen on completely deaf ears.

Even Susan, who had thought that Felicity had made a mistake in choosing to deal with Bonnie herself, had to admit that she had been wrong.

'Bonnie certainly seems to have turned over a new leaf,' she said now. 'And as for Veronica – well, she's like a completely different person. That's thanks to you as well.'

Felicity brushed this off with her usual modesty, yet she couldn't help but feel a small stirring of satisfaction as she watched Veronica laughing and joking with Pam and Nora in a way that would have been quite unimaginable a couple of weeks ago. Felicity had kept the promise she had made to herself, and spoken to Katherine of the fourth form about Veronica.

Fortunately, Katherine was a good-hearted girl and she agreed to persuade the fourth formers to make Veronica feel welcome when she joined them the next term.

'I never thought I would say this, but I shall actually miss Veronica when she moves up into the fourth,' said

Felicity. 'Now that she's put her spiteful ways behind her, she's really a nice person.'

'And she's got quite a sense of humour too,' said Susan. 'My goodness, I thought she was going to burst with laughter when Freddie and June played that trick on Mam'zelle Dupont yesterday.'

Veronica hadn't been the only one who had nearly burst, for the trick had been very funny indeed!

Freddie had waited until Susan took her book up to Mam'zelle's desk to have her work marked, then let out a piercing scream, which caused the French mistress to start violently, sending a shower of small blots over Susan's book.

'*Mon dieu!*' Mam'zelle cried angrily. 'Freddie, you bad girl! See what you have made me do? I have ruined the poor Susan's work. What is it that makes you scream like that?

'A s-spider!' Freddie stammered, making her eyes big and scared. 'I'm sorry that I startled you, Mam'zelle, but I do so hate spiders.'

In fact, Freddie wasn't scared of spiders at all, but Mam'zelle was, and she turned quite pale. 'Where did it go?' she asked, her voice quavering a little.

'It scuttled across the floor towards your desk, Mam'zelle,' Freddie answered.

Poor Mam'zelle looked most alarmed at this, her beady eyes rapidly scanning the floor around her desk.

'I see no spider,' Mam'zelle said at last. 'Freddie, if this is a trick . . .'

'It's no trick, Mam'zelle,' Nora piped up, very seriously. 'I saw it too. It was huge – almost as big as a mouse!'

Mam'zelle gave a little shriek, but Felicity said soothingly, 'It's all right, Mam'zelle. I think it escaped under the door and went out into the corridor.'

'Ah, thank goodness,' Mam'zelle sighed in relief, adding unnecessarily, 'Me, I do not like spiders. Susan, *ma chère*, I am sorry that I have spoiled your so-excellent work. You may go and sit down now.'

Susan, who knew that she had made several mistakes, was not at all sorry and went back to her seat thankfully. For the next few minutes the lesson progressed smoothly, then, when Mam'zelle turned to write something on the blackboard, Bonnie let out a loud squeal. Once again, Mam'zelle jumped, the chalk that she was holding skidding across the blackboard before she whirled round to face the class.

'The spider, Mam'zelle!' Bonnie squeaked, before the French mistress could speak. 'It's back! I saw it run up the leg of your desk.'

Mam'zelle leaped backwards, swaying on her high heels and almost overbalancing, causing Nora to let out one of her terrific snorts. Fortunately Mam'zelle was too preoccupied to hear it and she called out, 'June! You are not afraid of spiders. You are not afraid of *anything*! Come out here and search for the creature.'

So June, managing to keep her face remarkably straight, went over to Mam'zelle's desk and walked slowly around it, her expression so ridiculously solemn that it was too much for some of the girls. Felicity shook with silent laughter, while Pam and Julie had tears pouring down their cheeks. As for Veronica, her shoulders heaved as she struggled to control her mirth!

At last June said, 'I can't see the spider now, Mam'zelle. Perhaps I had better check inside your desk, to make sure that it's not hiding in there.'

Mam'zelle agreed to this at once, so June lifted the lid of the desk and rummaged around inside very thoroughly, making a lot of quite unnecessary noise as she poked in all the corners with a ruler. But no spider emerged and, feeling that it was safe to do so, Mam'zelle sent June back to her seat.

Then she almost collapsed into her own chair, saying, 'Poof! My heart, it goes pitter-pat! I have the palpitations!'

And she reached into the large, black handbag that she carried everywhere with her, pulling out her handkerchief so that she could mop her brow. But something else fell out of Mam'zelle's bag as well – the most enormous spider she had ever seen in her life! The girls had seen June slip it into the French mistress's bag as she pretended to look for the spider, but Mam'zelle hadn't. Poor Mam'zelle was also completely unaware that the spider wasn't real, but was, in fact, the rubber one that Alicia had sent to her cousin. It landed on the desk in front of her with a plop and, for a second, the French mistress could only stare helplessly at the enormous beast, frozen in terror. Then she jumped to her feet so suddenly that her chair crashed to the ground, and she let out a scream far louder than either Freddie's or Bonnie's had been.

'June!' she cried in anguish. 'Rescue me from this monster at once!'

June obliged immediately, bustling to the front of the class and putting her hand over the spider. 'Heavens, it's a big one!' she exclaimed. 'Are you sure you don't want to keep it as a pet, Mam'zelle?'

Mam'zelle was quite sure, shouting, 'It is *abominable*! Remove it at once, June, I beg of you!'

And, to the delight of the class, June picked up the spider by one of its legs, shaking her hand so that it looked as if the creature was trying to escape. Mam'zelle gave a shudder of revulsion, while the third formers, quite unable to contain their mirth now, laughed helplessly.

Unfortunately for them, Miss Potts was taking the first form in the neighbouring classroom, and had wondered what on earth could be going on next door. Eventually the noise had become so intrusive that she had hardly been able to hear herself speak, the first formers looking at one another in bewilderment.

This is too bad! Miss Potts thought to herself crossly. Mam'zelle must have left the room for a moment, and the third formers are taking advantage of her absence to play the fool. They really are old enough to know better!

And the mistress swept from the room, rapping sharply on the door of the third-form's classroom. However, the class was in such an uproar that no one even heard the knocking, so Miss Potts pushed open the door, halting on the threshold as her keen eyes took in the scene before her. There was Mam'zelle, in a state of great agitation, the girls reduced to tears of helpless laughter, and June, in the thick of the action – as usual!

'Mam'zelle!' she said loudly. 'What is the meaning of this?'

The mistress's stern voice and expression effectively sobered the third formers, and their laughter died away, as Mam'zelle cried, 'Ah, Miss Potts! There is a spider! As big as a man's fist. But the dear June, she has captured it.'

'Has she, indeed?' said Miss Potts drily, turning her steely gaze on the suddenly sheepish June. And, at once, Miss Potts saw what Mam'zelle hadn't – that the spider was a trick one.

'How brave of you, June,' she said sarcastically, before turning back to the French mistress. 'Mam'zelle, I should take a closer look at that spider, if I were you.'

With that, Miss Potts went out, shutting the door none too gently behind her, while Mam'zelle stared after her, half-indignant and half-puzzled. Had Miss Potts gone mad? Why should she, Mam'zelle, want to take a closer look at the spider? She wanted to get as far away from the spider as possible! She turned back to face the class, and suddenly realised that all the girls were looking rather apprehensive. Especially June, still standing in front of her desk holding the spider. A very still spider, which wasn't wriggling or moving at all now. All at once, the truth dawned on Mam'zelle – she had been tricked!

'June!' she snapped. 'You are a bad girl – you are all

bad girls, for you have tricked your poor Mam'zelle. Go to your seat now, and I shall decide what punishment to give you.'

The third formers were extremely subdued for the rest of the lesson, though every so often one or other of them couldn't help smiling as she remembered Mam'zelle's reaction to the spider. It would be a shame if they were punished, of course, but at the same time – what a super trick it had been!

At the end of the lesson, Mam'zelle stood up and looked round the class with sombre dark eyes. At last, she said heavily, 'I have decided on your punishment. You will all of you write me an essay in the holidays on the habits of spiders – in French!'

There was a gasp of dismay at this, as the girls looked at one another, aghast. They had *far* more important things to do in the holidays than write a beastly French essay! Didn't Mam'zelle realise that it was Christmas?

The French mistress looked with satisfaction at the expressions of horror on the girls' faces. Then a slow smile spread over her face, and she began to laugh. 'Hah!' she cried. 'Now it is I, Mam'zelle, who have tricked you! There will be no essay for you to do in the holidays. But you are all wicked girls, and your punishment will be to work twice as hard for me next term!'

'We will, Mam'zelle! We promise!' everyone called out at once, both relieved and delighted.

'Good old Mam'zelle!' chuckled Felicity as the girls filed out of the classroom.

'Yes, she's a real sport,' said Susan.

'And that was a simply first-rate trick, June and Freddie,' said Pam, grinning. 'My word, I thought I should die of laughter when that spider dropped on to Mam'zelle's desk.'

'Super!' agreed everyone.

As she recalled the trick now, Felicity said, with a little sigh, 'Oh, what fun we've had. I'm so looking forward to going home, and Christmas, and seeing my parents and Darrell. But I know that in a couple of weeks I shall be simply dying to get back to Malory Towers again.'

'I wonder if you'll see much of dear Bonnie during the holidays,' said Susan, and Felicity gave a groan.

The only thing marring her anticipation of the Christmas holidays was the thought that Bonnie would still be living down the road. The two of them had been getting along a lot better now that the air had been cleared between them, though it was obvious that Bonnie was happy with Amy as her friend and no longer worshipped Felicity. But the lingering fear that, when she was separated from Amy, Bonnie would cling to her again, would not go away. After all, one could never be *quite* sure what was going on in Bonnie's head!

But there was one final piece of good news for Felicity. Two days before the end of term, Bonnie came up to her, a letter in her hand.

'Guess what, Felicity?' she said. 'I've had a letter from Mummy – and we're moving! Daddy has got a job in another part of the country, so we're going to live there.

We shall be leaving a few days after Christmas.'

Felicity hardly knew what to say, but at last she managed, 'Well, I'm – er – I'm very sorry to hear that, Bonnie. I – um – I shall miss you.'

Bonnie looked hard at Felicity, then went off into a peal of laughter. 'No, you won't! You'll be jolly glad to see the back of me – admit it!'

Bonnie didn't seem at all offended, so Felicity grinned and said, 'I wouldn't go quite *that* far. You know, Bonnie you're not so bad really. You've just got some rather strange ideas about things!'

'So you keep telling me,' laughed Bonnie. 'Well, I shall be coming back to Malory Towers after the holidays, so perhaps then I shall learn how to be a proper Malory Towers schoolgirl!'

'Well, let's hope so,' said Pam later, when Felicity repeated this conversation. 'She does seem to have gained a *little* common sense just lately.'

'Yes, but I just hope her parents don't go and undo the good work we've done,' said Felicity. 'They're bound to thoroughly spoil her over Christmas.'

'And there's someone else who will be completely spoilt when she goes home,' said Julie as Amy walked by. 'I wonder what fabulous gifts Amy's parents are planning to bestow on her this Christmas!'

'Mrs Dale will keep her feet on the ground all right,' said Freddie. 'Or at any rate, she'll do her best to.'

'Well, jolly good luck to her,' said Nora, who wasn't particularly interested in Amy or Bonnie, but was looking forward to spending time with her own family. 'My word, only two days to go, then we shall be home! Where has the term gone?'

No one could answer that, but the next day flew by even faster, and then it was the last day.

The big entrance hall was very crowded and noisy as girls and mistresses said their goodbyes, invitations to Christmas parties were exchanged and parents who had come to collect their daughters joined the melee.

'Goodbye, Miss Peters! Goodbye, Mam'zelle Dupont!'

'Don't eat too much Christmas pudding, will you, Pam?'

'I'll see you at the pantomime on Boxing Day, Susan.'

'Felicity, your parents are here! They're outside.'

And it was time for Felicity to leave. She ran outside to greet her mother and father, stopping when she got to the big front door to say, 'Goodbye, Malory Towers – see you next term. I shall miss you!'

And we shall miss you, Felicity. But we'll see you again very soon.

EGMONT PRESS: ETHICAL PUBLISHING

Egmont Press is about turning writers into successful authors and children into passionate readers – producing books that enrich and entertain. As a responsible children's publisher, we go even further, considering the world in which our consumers are growing up.

Safety First
Naturally, all of our books meet legal safety requirements. But we go further than this; every book with play value is tested to the highest standards – if it fails, it's back to the drawing-board.

Made Fairly
We are working to ensure that the workers involved in our supply chain – the people that make our books – are treated with fairness and respect.

Responsible Forestry
We are committed to ensuring all our papers come from environmentally and socially responsible forest sources.

**For more information, please visit our website at
www.egmont.co.uk/ethical**